Messenger Bags and Murder

DOROTHY HOWELL

COVER ART BY STACY HOWELL

EDITED BY WILLIAM F. WU, PH.D.
WWW.WILLIAMFWU.COM

E-BOOK FORMATTING BY WEB CRAFTERS
WWW.WEBCRAFTERSDESIGN.COM

With love to Stacy, Judy, Brian, and Seth.

The author is extremely grateful for the love, support, and help of many people. Some of them are: Stacy Howell, Judith Branstetter, Brian Branstetter, Seth Branstetter, Martha Cooper, William F. Wu, Ph.D., and the talented people at Web Crafters Design.

Special thanks to Lisa Hammann, the winner of my Guess the Title Facebook contest.

BOOKLIST:

BOOKS BY DOROTHY HOWELL

The Haley Randolph Mystery Series
Handbags and Homicide
Purses and Poison
Shoulder Bags and Shootings
Clutches and Curses
Tote Bags and Toe Tags
Evening Bags and Executions
Beach Bags and Burglaries
Swag Bags and Swindlers
Slay Bells and Satchels
Duffel Bags and Drownings
Fanny Packs and Foul Play
Pocketbooks and Pistols
Backpacks and Betrayals
Messenger Bags and Murder

The Dana Mackenzie Mystery Series
Fatal Debt
Fatal Luck
Fatal Choice

ROMANCES BY JUDITH STACY

Outlaw Love
The Marriage Mishap
The Heart of a Hero
The Dreammaker
The Blushing Bride
Written in the Heart

The Last Bride in Texas
The Nanny
Married by Midnight
Cheyenne Wife
The Widow's Little Secret
Maggie and the Law
The One Month Marriage
The Hired Husband
Jared's Runaway Woman
Christmas Wishes
Wild West Wager
"Three Brides and a Wedding Dress" in Spring Brides
"A Place to Belong" in Stay for Christmas
"Courting Miss Perfect" in Stetsons, Spring, and Wedding Rings
"Texas Cinderella" in Happily Ever After in the West
"Waiting for Christmas" in All a Cowboy Wants for Christmas

ROMANCES BY DOROTHY HOWELL
Defiant Enchantress
Anna's Treasure
Tea Time

CHAPTER ONE

"He said *what?*" Marcie screamed.

I pulled my cell phone away from my ear, not surprised by her reaction—the only reaction possible from my BFF.

"Oh, my God, you're kidding me," she went on. "You're totally kidding me. Tell me you're kidding me."

I didn't bother answering because I knew she wasn't ready to hear anything more—that's how huge the news was that I'd just shared with her.

I was walking down the hallway toward the office of L.A. Affairs where I, Haley Randolph, with my I-look-smart-because-I'm-a-brunette dark hair, and my long they're-the-only-thing-I-inherited-from-my-beauty-queen-mom pageant legs, worked as an event planner. It was Monday morning and, somehow, I was actually running a little ahead of schedule.

Weird, especially for a Monday.

"I don't believe this," Marcie ranted. "I absolutely do not believe this."

The hallway was crowded with well-dressed men and women juggling briefcases, messenger bags, handbags, totes, and coffee in to-go cups, everybody scrambling to get wherever they were going. The building was located on the fashionable corner of Sepulveda and Ventura in prestigious Sherman Oaks, one of Los Angeles's most sought-after locations. Everybody seemed anxious to get to their desk, hunker down, and surge into the week with renewed vigor.

Except for me.

But I had a good excuse.

I heard Marcie draw a huge breath and let it out slowly, a sign that she was winding down.

"Okay," she said. "We've got to get together tonight. I have to hear everything. *Everything*."

"I'll text you," I promised.

We ended the call as I pushed through the door of L.A. Affairs bracing myself, as usual, for the ridiculous *are you ready to party* chant our receptionist Mindy always hit me with as if I were a potential client, not an employee. I kept my head down, determined to ignore her, but when I didn't hear anything I glanced up. A woman I'd never seen before sat behind the reception desk.

Okay, that was weird. Mindy had never—ever—missed a day of work.

Tempted as I was to ask what the heck was going on, I decided to just roll with it. It was Monday, I was early, and I'd just shared colossal news with Marcie. I didn't think I could take anything else right now.

I headed past the client interview rooms and the cube farm, then turned down the hallway where the offices and conference room were located, and went into my private office. I loved my office—neutral furniture with splashes of blue and yellow, and huge windows that offered a great view of the Galleria shopping center across the street.

It was a new day, a new week, abounding with new opportunities. Conscientious workers all over the world would immediately dig in, get organized, set priorities, and formulate a plan for the day.

I wasn't one of those people.

I dropped my handbag—a classic Chanel satchel I'd paired with my even-on-a-Monday-I-dress-to-kill black business suit—in the bottom drawer of my desk and headed for the breakroom. But before I'd taken two steps I spotted a large sheet of paper taped to my computer screen, with something written on it in red marker.

Okay, that was weird.

Weird, even for a Monday.

I looked closer. *Report to my office immediately*, was printed in huge block letters, the last word underlined three times. It was signed by Priscilla.

Priscilla was the office manager.

Okay, that was really weird.

She wanted me front and center with such urgency that she hadn't sent a text, a DM, an email, or left me a voice mail? She'd actually handwritten a sign, walked to my office, and taped it to my computer? First thing? On a Monday morning?

Yikes!

Immediately, I launched into full panic mode.

Oh my God. *Oh my God.* What was going on? Why was Priscilla apparently on fire to see me? Was I in major trouble?

My thoughts raced backward. I couldn't think of anything I'd done wrong—well, okay, there was that one thing. But that was it—no, hang on, there was that other thing, too. But Priscilla couldn't have found out about them—not this quickly.

I drew in a few breaths trying to calm myself—I don't really like being calm—because I couldn't report to Priscilla's office this rattled. For a moment I considered grabbing a client portfolio and rushing out on a made-up appointment, but I'm not big on suspense. No way did I want this thing—whatever it was—hanging over my head all day. I was going to march into Priscilla's office and find out what the heck was going on.

As soon as I fortified myself with some chocolate and caffeine.

I hurried to the breakroom. It was crowded with employees—all female, all dressed in magnificent clothing—and wormed my way to the coffee pot on the counter, the office hotspot for gossip, speculation, and hearing—or starting—rumors.

Conversation flowed around me as I poured myself a cup and pretended this was just an average Monday morning. I didn't hear anyone mention being called to Priscilla's office.

I dumped several sugars into my coffee and hit it with a huge blast of French vanilla creamer, then stood around listening as other employees flowed in and out of the breakroom. Still, no one mentioned anything major going down, or news of a suspected lay-off or someone getting fired, or anyone else getting summoned to Priscilla's office.

Oh, my God. Was I the only one?

Apparently so.

I finished my coffee but no way was I mentally prepared to face whatever awaited me. I grabbed a package of M&Ms from the snack cabinet, dumped it in my mouth, and left the breakroom.

The hallway was empty as I headed toward Priscilla's office. My brain was hopping, thanks to the major chocolate infusion, which was good. No doubt I'd have to mentally bob and weave my way through whatever awaited.

Up ahead I spotted Kayla, my L.A. Affairs' BFF. She was about my age—mid-twenties—with dark hair and a curvy figure. We were both event planners, spending our days organizing and executing the these-people-are-nuts events that our clientele of Hollywood insiders, the rich, famous, and power players of Los Angeles, demanded.

Since Kayla was my BFF, normally I would immediately spout off about being called to Priscilla's office. But I couldn't bring myself to say anything—not yet, not until I knew what I was in for. I mean, really, if I was about to be fired I didn't want that rumor whipping through the office—not until I'd first started the rumor that I'd learned a heinous secret about Priscilla and had resigned on moral grounds.

"How's it going?" I said, trying to sound casual.

"Good," Kayla said, sounding just as casual. "You?"

"Great," I said.

"I'm great, too," Kayla insisted.

We both stood there for a moment until I noticed we were a few feet away from Priscilla's office. She seemed to realize it at the same instant.

"Did you get—" she asked.

"Yes," I said. "Did you?"

"Yes! Oh, my God, what's going on?"

We were both in high panic mode. Obviously, we were in this together—which was good because that left us the entire office to blame everything on.

"I have no idea what this is about," Kayla said.

"Me either," I swore. "I haven't had any problems with anyone or anything."

"Neither have I," she insisted.

Of course, we were both lying—but it was good practice for when we got into Priscilla's office.

Priscilla suddenly appeared in the doorway, her mouth open, drawing in a big breath as if she was readying to yell, then spotted us.

"Oh. There you are. Come in, come in." Priscilla waved us forward with both hands.

She looked awesome, as always, dressed in a terrific suit, her makeup and nails done, her hair in a chic style. I considered her a good office manager, mostly because she left me alone to do my job and usually believed whatever b.s. I found it necessary to bestow upon her. I didn't know what the heck was up with her today. I'd never seen her this frazzled.

"Sit down, sit down." She closed the door behind us.

Kayla and I dropped into the chairs in front of the desk and exchanged a troubled look. A closed door and an insistence that we sit were not good signs. The only saving grace was that Edie, the Human Resources manager, wasn't here—not yet, anyway.

Priscilla curled one leg under her and sat down, leaned forward with both elbows on her desk, and twisted her fingers together. "Something's come up."

It wasn't her you're-in-trouble voice, more like the universal someone-has-died voice. I didn't know whether to be more—or less—upset.

"This morning, Rachel and Sienna were in a car accident," Priscilla said.

Rachel and Sienna were senior event planners with L.A. Affairs. I knew them well enough to make small talk in the breakroom, but that was it.

Priscilla rushed on. "It was minor—well, somewhat minor. Neither was seriously injured, but both have been taken to the hospital for treatment. This has left us in a lurch."

Okay, so obviously this wasn't something awful directed at me. I wasn't about to be fired, or reprimanded, or anything. But I did feel kind of weird realizing that I'd never even considered that being called to Priscilla's office might be something good—which says a lot about the way my life had been going lately.

"You want Haley and me to take over their events until they get back?" Kayla asked.

"No." Priscilla seemed to spin up even more, bobbing up and down in her chair, twisting her fingers harder. "Rachel and Sienna were enroute to HPA, the annual premiere gathering of hospitality industry professionals from across the country. The week-long event is highly exclusive. Only the very best in the field have even a small glimmer of hope that they will be included. Hospitality Professionals of America is extremely prestigious. I don't know if you've heard about it."

My senses jumped to high alert. I'd heard rumors of HPA, but I didn't think it was real, more like a myth. Sort of like Asgard and Atlantis—and four-inch heels that were comfortable.

"This is the first year L.A. Affairs was extended an invitation." Priscilla plastered both palms on her desk. "And now *this*."

Kayla and I exchanged another look. I didn't know where this was going and, apparently, neither did she.

"It's imperative that we have a presence at the event. To cancel at this hour ...." Priscilla shook her head. "It's unthinkable."

Hospitality companies lived or died by their reputations. If L.A. Affairs couldn't manage to get two of their own employees to a conference, how would that look? Everybody would question whether the company was capable to staging high profile events. Word would spread. Other companies and clients would be reluctant to book anything through us. Our image would suffer massively.

"Therefore ..." Priscilla paused, gulped, and drew herself up. "It's been determined that you two should represent L.A. Affairs at the event."

Kayla and I exchanged yet another look, this one a this-is-too-good-to-be-true look.

"I know, I know," Priscilla said, twisting her fingers together again. "There are other senior planners here. More experienced. Higher profile planners. But, because of the caliber of events they're executing at the moment, they can't possibly attend the conference, can't possibly be unavailable to their clients for the entire week. So, there is nothing left to do, no other option available, but to send the two of you."

Oh my God, I was having my own personal *Top Gun* moment. Just like Maverick and Goose when they were selected to go to the flying competition after the first guys couldn't make it, the place where only the best of the best got to go. Kayla and I were in those roles.

I, of course, was Maverick.

"HPA is being held at the Severin Retreat and Conference Center near Santa Barbara." Priscilla leaned forward. "You must—you absolutely must—leave immediately. The launch activities begin this afternoon."

"What about our events?" Kayla asked, gesturing to me. "The ones we're handling for our clients?"

Okay, like I cared about the parties and luncheons I was organizing when I had a cool opportunity like this?

No way could I say that, of course.

"All of my events are handled," I said, which was true. Actually, I'm really good at this job.

"Mine, too," Kayla said. "But what if something comes up? I can't abandon my clients."

"Me, either," I said. Of course, I could, but I didn't want to say so.

"I'll have another planner monitor the progress and get in touch with you immediately if problems arise." Priscilla rose from her chair and waved her hand at her computer. "I'll send you the itinerary and other pertinent information."

Kayla and I popped up out of our chairs.

"We'll go home, pack, and hit the road," Kayla said.

"I'll expect updates throughout the day, every day, from each of you." Priscilla turned to me with semi-stink eye. "*Each* of you."

"No problem," I said.

I made a move to leave but Priscilla kept staring at us.

"This is a rare opportunity for L.A. Affairs to move into the upper echelon of the hospitality industry. Let me emphasize again how important HPA is to the future of our company," Priscilla said, and swallowed hard. "And it's in your hands."

"We won't let you down," Kayla told her, with a confident smile.

Priscilla didn't smile back. Actually, she looked as if she were feeling kind of sick.

"We're going now," Kayla said.

I followed her out of the office, then looked back. Priscilla collapsed into her chair, planted her elbows on her desk, dropped her face into her palms and shook her head wildly.

"Let's get out of here," Kayla whispered.

"Hell, yeah," I murmured.

The only bump in the road ahead of me was my promise to Marcie that I would tell her *everything* at dinner tonight. It would have to wait. It suited me better, really. I kind of wanted to forget the whole thing for a while anyway.

I headed for my office, my spirits high, my steps light, *Highway to the Danger Zone* playing in my head. Now, instead of slogging through my daily grind, I was off to a fantastic retreat for a whole week.

What a heck of a way to start off a Monday.

No way could anything bad happen now.

No way.

CHAPTER TWO

"Oh my God, everybody who's anybody is going to be at this thing," Kayla said, studying her phone and the info Priscilla had sent.

We'd both rushed home, packed, I'd picked her up, and we were now headed north on the 101 toward Santa Barbara.

"Yeah?" I asked. "Who?"

The freeway hugged the coast and we were treated to awesome views of the ocean on our left, and the rugged mountains on our right. The sky was blue, the sun bright, the weather awesome, as expected in Southern California.

And, as expected, Kayla and I looked pretty awesome, as well, still dressed in our killer business suits. Even though this event was taking place at a retreat, apparently no one was allowed to actually relax. According to the info Priscilla had provided, business attire was expected until after dinner, when standards were slightly downgraded to dressy business casual.

Kayla swiped through her phone. "All the most prestigious companies will be there. I've never even heard of some of them."

I'd glanced over the information about the conference earlier, but only enough to find out what I should pack for the week. My most fashion-forward business suits were now in a garment bag, and my suitcase held shoes, accessories, and my stunning, look-at-me-and-be-jealous array of designer handbags.

I've completely lost my mind over designer handbags. I absolutely must have the hottest, coolest, trendiest, of-the-moment purse, and I'd go to any lengths to get it. Really, any lengths.

Some people say I have a problem; I say it's no problem at all.

"The convention center looks awesome. They've got all kinds of amenities, including their own vineyard and a helipad. You can tell they're shooting for big-money clients," Kayla said, swiping more screens on her phone. "It looks like this week's schedule will have a huge lineup of classes for all sorts of hospitality products and services."

I wasn't a big fan of attending classes—I tended to drift off—because they all pretty much seemed alike—mind-numbing and butt-flattening. Maybe I could find a way to get out of most of them.

"Catering, lighting, music, flowers, table linens, and candles," Kayla went on. "Selecting venues, hiring security and construction companies. Furniture and seating. There'll be vendors and an exhibit hall."

I perked up a little. Oddly enough, all of that stuff sounded interesting to me. I actually liked my job.

"Oh, wow, and get this," Kayla said. "They're giving away messenger bags. Five of them. From a designer named Carlo Casale. Have you heard of him?"

"What?"

I nearly swerved into the other lane.

Oh my God, Carlo Casale—I think he's Italian, but if he's not he should be—was simultaneously the hottest and the coolest designer in the entire world. His bags were to die for, sought after by absolutely everyone and, of course, impossible to find. His latest messenger bag had been featured in all the fashion magazines and on the trendiest websites. I'd fallen in love with it—and become obsessed with it—the moment I'd seen it.

"Is it the Titan messenger bag?" I asked. Actually, I might have shouted that.

Casale's latest line was the Galaxy collection. Each item was named for a planet, or a star, or a nebula, or something—I don't know, I get all of those things mixed up. All I knew for sure was that Titan was Saturn's largest moon because I'd read it in a *Vogue* magazine ad. The gist of the whole thing was that if you carried a Casale bag your career would soar—the galaxy was the limit, not simply the sky.

Cool, huh?

"Yeah, it's the Titan. The bags are a giveaway," Kayla said. "Friday, to close the event."

To make sure nobody left early, no doubt.

I hate it when that happens.

"What kind of giveaway? A random drawing? Some sort of conference participation criteria?" I asked, my mind buzzing through all the things I'd do to get one of those bags, then deciding, of course, I'd do *anything* to get one.

We've all got our priorities.

"It doesn't say," Kayla said and flipped to the next screen on her phone.

Obviously, Kayla wasn't as crazed over the Titan messenger bags as I was, but that's okay. I could still be friends with her. I was all about diversity.

"I think you know this guy," she said and tapped on her phone. "Jack Bishop."

I nearly swerved into the other lane again.

Oh my God, Jack would be there? At the conference? The one I was also attending? We'd be there together for an entire week?

Jack was a private investigator who was even hotter and cooler than Carlo Casale—but in a totally different way. Jack owned his own security firm. I'd met him a while back when I was employed at an L.A. badass law firm and Jack had done some consulting for them. Since then we'd worked together on cases. The heat between us was undeniable but it had never gone anywhere. I'd been involved with someone else, and I'm a one-man-at-a-time kind of gal—no exceptions. Jack always respected that—sort of.

"I've seen him in the office," Kayla said. "He's really hot."

"I've hired his firm for some of my events," I said and managed to sound calm even though my thoughts were racing. "He does a first-class job."

"He's handling security at the conference, and it's his first time there," Kayla said, gesturing to her phone. "Wow, that firm of his must be awesome, if he got this gig."

It didn't get bigger than HPA. This was a high-visibility opportunity that would elevate Jack's business and bring in tons more clients. I knew he'd do a great job.

Kayla went on about the week's events but, honestly, I wasn't really listening until my GPS intruded on my thoughts and announced my freeway exit was coming up. I followed the streets that rose into the hills above Santa Barbara, then turned onto a road marked with a discreet sign—meant to keep out the riff-raff, I suspect—that wound through a wooded area.

The Severin Retreat and Conference Center appeared as we crested a rise, making it seem as if we'd somehow time-traveled to ancient Greece. The huge building was made of white stone and had tons of columns, statues, and carvings that gave it an elegant and dignified look in a restrained way that screamed don't-think-for-a-minute-you're-actually-going-to-have-a-good-time-here. A perfectly manicured lawn stretched out in front of the building dotted with fountains and gardens of artfully arranged flowers. Down a shallow incline was a small lake with—and, really, I'm not kidding here—swans.

A team of valets in cream-colored jackets and blue bow ties descended on us when I pulled to a stop, and made quick work of unloading our bags as a young woman in a cream-colored business suit—cream being as wild as it got at Severin, apparently—approached.

"Welcome," she said, clutching a tablet and wearing an I-get-paid-to-be-this-friendly smile. "I'm Shannon Alda, your personal hostess."

She was petite, with blonde hair and blue eyes. I figured she was a couple of years younger than me, likely a recent graduate with a degree in hospitality who'd impressed somebody enough to score a job at a prestigious place like Severin. She looked composed, confident, and capable, and seemed to be on top of things because she already knew our names.

"I was so sorry to learn about Rachel and Sienna," Shannon said, as we headed toward the building's entrance. "Do you have an update on their hospitalization?"

Actually, I'd forgotten all about them—which was bad, I know. But I'd had all kinds of other stuff on my mind, little of which had anything to do with L.A. Affairs or the HPA conference.

Luckily, Kayla held her phone in her hand, as if she had a hotline to the hospital, and said, "There's been no change."

"Everyone is so relieved you two could step in at the last minute," Shannon said.

She ushered us inside. The lobby was huge—really, you could have played a pro baseball game in here.

Cream was the go-to color. It had been accessorized with varying shades of blue, a good choice for the month of January when it was too early for pastels, and the reds and oranges of the holidays brought back too many thank-God-we-survived memories. The ceiling featured a series of domes, each painted with scenes of nearly naked cherubs and plump adults wrapped in strategically placed scarves, frolicking on clouds. The check-in desk stretched along the far wall and was backed by a mural of green meadows, trees, flowers, and grazing sheep.

A number of conference attendees were scattered throughout the lobby, seated in groups, and huddled in knots. Everyone wore their finest business attire and was perfectly groomed. There was a little commotion nearby where a woman was leading another woman around as if she were a dog on a leash, presenting her to everyone they passed. Otherwise, conversation was low, voices muted.

Shannon did a series of modified Vanna White moves—discreet gestures, as per the Severin employee handbook, no doubt—and pointed to the right where the main corridor led to the exhibit hall and the meeting and conference rooms, then to our left where the guest rooms were located.

"Your bags are being sent to your room," Shannon said, tapping on her tablet. "Since you're new to the conference this year, you're in the first group for the labyrinth walk. It's a timed departure. I'm sending you the link now with all the information."

Kayla and I pulled out our phones and I saw that, already, I'd received a text from Priscilla wanting an update. Jeez, did she really think something text-worthy had happened already?

I didn't respond. I had something really important that required my immediate attention.

"I understand the conference has the Titan messenger bags?" I asked, and managed to sound calm and controlled.

Shannon's half-frozen, Severin-regulation smile amped up. "Oh, yes, and they're gorgeous. One of them is on display. Would you like to see it?"

It took everything I had not to push through the crowd, elbows-out to clear a path, but I managed to channel my beauty pageant mother's I'm-better-than-you attitude and walked sedately alongside Shannon. Kayla might have said something. I don't know. I wasn't listening.

We entered the massive exhibit hall. The space was filled with vendor booths. Conference attendees roamed the aisles, chatting with the booth monitors, looking things over, picking up brochures.

Shannon stopped and gestured to a large display stand positioned prominently near the entry. Upon it, enclosed in a glass case, sat a Titan messenger bag.

Someone moaned. I thought it was Shannon, but I'm afraid it was actually me.

How could I not? The bag bore the signature fabric and distinctive logo that all Casale items were known for. And it was gorgeous—no, actually, it was beyond gorgeous.

I paused in humble reverence, giving myself a moment to take it in. I didn't trust myself to get too close yet, fearing I might actually lick the glass. Somehow, I pulled myself together—I can push through when I have to—and joined Shannon and Kayla at the display.

"The giveaway bags are carefully stored. They're filled with swag, but not this one, of course," Shannon said. "The Casale rep felt the swag would alter the shape and the crisp lines of the display bag since it's positioned upright in the case. She felt it would diminish its desirability."

Oh my God, a Casale rep had been here? And might return? Wow, this conference was getting better and better.

"The HPA participants have been extremely generous with their swag donations, awarding the most desirable goods and services their firms offer," Shannon said.

14

"Like the Oscar and Emmy swag bags?" Kayla asked.

"And just as valuable. See for yourself." Shannon circled the display stand, then frowned. "There's a brochure with all the details. It should be here."

As if on cue, a hot-looking guy wearing a Severin polo shirt—cream colored, of course—hurried over pushing a cart loaded with cardboard boxes.

"Just got these from the printer—again," he said, and started unloading brochures from one of the boxes. He passed one to each of us and gave a decidedly un-Severin-like eye roll. "One of the vendors insisted on a change."

The brochure was a slick tri-fold with the Titan messenger bag on the front. Inside was a list of the vendors who'd contributed swag. Everything had been selected to appeal to hospitality industry professionals, an enticement to try out their services and then recommend them to wealthy clients for their high-profile events.

"Thanks, Zander," Shannon said.

He emptied the box, gave her a friendly nod, and walked away with the cart.

My eyes widened as I read the list of vendor-donated swag. This was awesome. Trips and cruises, discounted use of venues, free products and services. I noted that L.A. Affairs had jumped on the try-us-on-the-cheap bandwagon, offering the services of one of our event planners at no cost. I wondered who would get stuck doing that.

"This is a spectacular giveaway," Kayla said, flipping through the brochure.

"It's impressive," Shannon agreed, looking over the list. "The swag alone is valued at—"

She paused, blinked rapidly at the brochure, then pressed her lips together and frowned.

"Well, yes, the giveaway is stunning," she said, drawing in a breath. "Enjoy the conference." She hurried away, yanking her phone out of her pocket.

"I guess the value of the swag is some sort of secret," Kayla said.

"Yeah, and we almost heard it."

I hate it when that happens.

"We'd better go," Kayla said, checking the time on her phone. "We can't miss our turn in the labyrinth walk."

I had no idea what a labyrinth walk was, but I figured somebody would explain it when we got there. I took one last lingering look at the Titan messenger bag, and left.

Luckily, Kayla had read over the info Shannon had sent so she led the way. Outside she gestured toward the vineyard, helipad, tennis courts, and swimming pool as we followed a long walkway that took us away from the conference center and wound through a wooded area. Trees, flowers, and shrubs were plentiful, and placed among them were benches, statues, and fountains. Twinkle lights and accent lighting lit the path, since the sun was almost down.

Up ahead I spotted a woman dressed in a white flowing dress with a wreath of flowers in her graying hair, standing next to some tall shrubs. She swayed back and forth to music that, apparently, played only in her head, as she raised her outstretched arms skyward.

"What the heck?" I mumbled. "Can we ditch this?"

"I wish. Priscilla has texted twice to make sure we're following the conference schedule," Kayla whispered back. "She wants pictures."

So far the labyrinth walk wasn't screaming *party-on*, but it seemed we had no choice.

The woman dressed like an aging fairy stopped swaying as we approached.

"Welcome. You may call me Bliss," she crooned and waved her hands toward the trees that surrounded us. "You are indeed here on a most special evening. The full moon will light your way to internal peace and tranquility as you walk through our labyrinth."

I glanced up and saw that the treetops shone with yellow light as the moon peaked over.

"What is this? A maze?" I asked, looking at the flagstone path that disappeared through the double row of tall shrubs.

"Oh, no." Bliss shook her head and favored us with a dreamy smile. "In a maze you could become lost and wander aimlessly looking for your destination. In our labyrinth you'll simply follow the path, and along the way you'll find internal peace and tranquility."

I figured having some internal peace and tranquility in my life wouldn't hurt anything, although usually I wasn't a big fan of it. The moon over the treetops did look pretty, plus all the flowers made the air smell sweet. And, if we got this over quickly, we could go do something that was actual fun.

"The labyrinth on the full moon offers a centering effect that puts us in touch with the wisdom of our bodies," Bliss went on, and started swaying again for no apparent reason. "It's the moment when we must slow down, become aware of the sky, the air, the scent of the earth and all it offers."

Kayla and I shared a what-the-heck look.

"Please take a moment to center yourselves and relax your minds, while those ahead of you finish their walk." Bliss said. "Our retreat values silence, stillness, and a quiet reflective atmosphere."

We stepped to the side and Bliss started swaying again.

"Rachel and Sienna are lucky they missed this," I murmured.

"They probably crashed their car on purpose," Kayla whispered back.

Wish I'd thought of that.

The low hum of voices floated through the air. I looked back down the walkway and saw three women headed toward the labyrinth, and behind them were two more groups of people. If we didn't get moving we'd be stacked up like aircraft over LAX waiting to land.

Bliss must have realized that, too, because she gestured grandly to the labyrinth entrance.

"Walk at your leisure. You'll easily see the exit and the path back to the conference center," she said. "May you have a journey of self-discovery that brings you joy and peace."

Kayla and I paused in front of the tall shrubs, snapped selfies for Priscilla, and headed into the labyrinth. The walkway was just wide enough for us to walk side-by-side and the shrubs that bordered it were taller than me, giving it a tunnel effect. Moonbeams lit the way, along with minimal lighting that ran alongside the path.

"Are you feeling any internal peace yet?" Kayla asked, as we followed the curving trail.

"No," I said.

"How about tranquility?" she asked.

"Not a bit," I said.

"I say we look for some tranquility at the bar."

I couldn't disagree.

We picked up our pace and followed the winding route until we finally spotted a break in the wall of shrubs up ahead.

"The exit. Thank God," Kayla said. "Let's get out of here."

But as we drew closer, I saw something lying across the path just outside the labyrinth.

I got a weird feeling.

It was a woman. Moonbeams highlighted blood and yucky stuff that covered a big smashed-in spot on her head.

Oh, crap.

No way was I feeling any internal peace or tranquility now.

She was dead.

CHAPTER THREE

"Oh my God," Kayla gasped. "Is she—"

"Yes."

"—dead?"

"Yes."

"Dead?"

The woman lay just steps outside the labyrinth exit, sprawled across the path and onto the grass. Blood pooled around her and glistened in her blonde hair from the huge dent in her skull.

"Murdered," I said.

"Murdered? Are you—are you … sure?" Kayla asked.

Obviously, this was Kayla's first homicide. Wish I could say the same for myself.

"Do you know who she is?" I asked.

"What? No."

We both hesitated a moment, then leaned a little closer. I figured the woman for mid-40s, trim, dressed in a well-accessorized, bright red pantsuit that I knew immediately was by Zac Posen.

Kayla gasped again. "I saw her. In the conference center. Oh my God. She was with that celebrity chef. You saw them, too."

"I did?"

"The chef from the TV show. She was just named champion of one of those cooking competitions." Panic crept into Kayla's voice. "Oh my God. They were together. Is that chef dead, too?"

Kayla was on the edge of losing it—not that I blamed her—so I caught her arm and turned her away from the body.

"Go back through the labyrinth," I said. "If you see anybody, make them to go back—but don't tell them why, just say somebody is sick. We don't want anybody to panic. Then tell what's-her-name at the entrance not to send anybody else through."

She gulped hard, gave me a quick nod, and hurried away.

I stepped through the labyrinth exit—careful not to disturb anything—and looked around. The wooded area had been left pretty much in its natural state; nothing had been trimmed, cut, or sculpted. The only lighting was along the walkway back to the conference center and the moonlight that filtered through the tall trees. Nothing moved. No sign of the possibly dead celebrity chef.

I called Jack.

My call went to voicemail. I hung up and called back. Jack always answered my calls. I hoped his failure to pick up meant he was doing something fun, because I was pretty sure it would be the last fun thing that would happen to him this week.

My call went to voicemail again. I called back.

It was Jack's first time at the conference, the first time his company was providing security here. He'd scored a huge opportunity. And somebody had been murdered on his watch.

Not good.

Jack picked up.

"I can't talk now," he said in a hushed voice. "I'm dealing with something."

"I know. I'm at the conference, too," I told him. "You found out what happened already? Wow. Impressive."

"If stolen messenger bags are my biggest problem this week, I can relax."

"Messenger bags? What are you talking—oh my God, the Titan messenger bags were stolen?" I might have said that kind of loud.

Jack didn't respond. I felt the tension coming through my phone.

"Talk to me, Haley," he finally said. "Are stolen messenger bags my biggest problem? Can I relax?"

"I wouldn't wait for internal peace or tranquility," I said. "You've got a really big problem."

***

"That's her." Kayla turned her phone toward me. "Rosalind Russo, the celebrity chef."

We were seated in the conference center bar drinking wine—which we both really deserved, after the labyrinth walk. I'd waited until Jack and two of his guys showed up, and hung around long enough to give him a quick rundown of what had happened. No way did I want to be there when the homicide detectives and crime scene techs showed up.

"It was the Comfort Food Championship. Six weekly challenges on one of the food networks. The series is huge," Kayla said.

The bar was busy but quiet—even here everyone spoke in a low voice.

"Rosalind won," she said. "The show just aired. See?"

I watched on Kayla's phone as confetti rained down on a group of apron-clad contestants in a faux kitchen, forcing we're-on-camera-so-we-have-to-look-like-good-sports smiles. In the center was Rosalind Russo tearfully laughing while looking genuinely surprised and modest. She was probably mid-thirties, with brown hair twisted in a neat up-do, and a waistline that indicated she'd put a lot of effort into tasting her own creations.

"I saw Rosalind with the ... the victim," Kayla said, and knocked back her wine again. "When Shannon showed us the Titan messenger bag. You must have noticed them."

My thoughts spun back until they landed on the woman in the bright red pantsuit I'd spotted as she worked the room; Rosalind had been alongside her.

"So what's Rosalind doing *here*?" I asked, and sipped my wine. "Wouldn't the network have all sorts of publicity lined up for her? Flashier publicity than this place? I mean, really, a conference appearance for a TV celebrity?"

"You'd think," Kayla said and laid her phone aside. "Do you suppose we'll have to talk to the police about ... you know?"

I was ready to launch into my this-is-how-you-talk-to-homicide-detectives speech, but I was afraid it would create questions that I didn't want to answer.

"We saw nothing, so there's nothing much to tell them," I pointed out.

"Yeah, I guess." Kayla gulped down the rest of her wine and signaled the server for another. She fidgeted for a moment, then said, "So that means somebody here is a murderer."

Her gaze darted around the room full of strangers, and I knew what she was thinking. But there was nothing I could say to make her feel better. I wasn't feeling so great myself.

"Are we safe here?" Kayla asked. "Your friend who's handling security, Jack. He knows what he's doing?"

"He does," I said. "And the police have started investigating already."

The server brought Kayla's wine. She drained half the glass.

"Do you think they'll cancel the conference?" she asked.

"More likely they'll ignore the whole thing. No way would HPA or Severin want any negative publicity," I said.

"But shouldn't they say something to *us*?" Kayla asked. "We found a *dead body* on their grounds."

It did seem kind of weird that Shannon, our personal hostess, hadn't sought us out to offer an apology, or an explanation—or made some kind of overture that might head off a lawsuit. I mean, jeez, we could have at least been offered a complimentary cheese tray or something.

"They'll pretend like it's nothing? Just sweep it under the rug?" Kayla looked majorly rattled, and the numerous glasses of wine she'd consumed didn't seem to be helping.

"Are you going to be okay here?" I asked. "Do you want to leave?"

"Do you?" she asked, as if she hoped I did so we could grab our bags and make a run for it.

"I don't think we're in any danger," I said.

She drained her glass. "But what if the—the murderer saw us at the labyrinth exit? What if whoever did it thinks we can identify him?"

Yeah, well, okay, there's that.

Jeez, trying to sound reasonable and comforting was taking its toll on me.

"Look," I said. "If you're afraid and you want to leave, you should call Priscilla."

Kayla mumbled a curse, then moaned. "Priscilla. You know she'll tell Edie, and Edie will plaster it all over my personnel file. Priscilla will hold it against me forever if I leave and throw shade over the reputation of L.A. Affairs. She'll assign me every crappy event that comes along."

Yeah, Kayla would likely end up being the office radiation canary, and neither of us wanted that to happen.

"So let's not mention anything to Priscilla, or anyone at L.A. Affairs," I said.

Priscilla had been so wound up when we left the office this morning I figured learning now that Kayla and I had been involved with a murder—no matter how innocently—might push Priscilla into a full blown stroke. No way did I want that noted in my permanent record.

"Okay." Kayla nodded. "I guess nothing bad can happen for the rest of the conference, after this."

She hadn't been with me when I'd phoned Jack and he'd told me the Titan messenger bags had been stolen, so she didn't know that something else bad had already happened. No way was I telling her—or anyone else at the conference. I'd seen that the bag in the display case in the exhibit hall was still in place when we got back from the labyrinth so, hopefully, the theft of the other four bags could be kept quiet. It was a break for Jack and his security team.

"So," Kayla began, as if she were anxious to move on to a different topic of conversation. "Did you have to put any major plans on hold to come up here this week?"

"Nothing on hold," I said, and finished my wine.

I had put something major on *ignore*, though. That whole situation with my ex-official boyfriend Ty Cameron—the one Marcie had nearly lost her mind over when I'd told her about my last conversation with him on the phone this morning on my way into the office—would have to be dealt with. I wasn't anxious to tackle the subject. Being here at the conference was a good excuse to avoid the whole thing.

Still, the image of tall, handsome Ty sped through my brain. His family had owned the Holt's Department Store chain for five generations, which was where we'd met when I took a job as a sales clerk there last year—long story. Our relationship wasn't exactly as smooth as silk PJs over freshly shaved legs. We'd decided to break up—no, actually, Ty made the decision and I'd gone along with it. Then he left. For three months. Three months without a call, a text, an email. Nothing. Then he showed up at my apartment.

"You didn't have anything going on this week?" Kayla asked. "Aren't you still dating that lawyer?"

Yes, of course, I was dating Liam Douglas—and I hadn't forgotten about him. Really.

Liam was tall, with blonde hair and gorgeous eyes, and a good build. He was handsome, funny, smart, and not only listened when I told him things but actually remembered what I'd said. Our relationship was moving at Grandma-on-a-walker speed, but so far it was working for both of us.

"Liam and I are still together," I said. "In fact, I have a date with him—"

Oh, crap.

I had a date scheduled with him tonight—*tonight*—and I'd totally forgotten to tell him I'd left town. But that could have happened to anybody. Right? It didn't mean something was wrong with our relationship. Right?

Well, okay, maybe it did.

No time to think about that now.

I hopped out of the chair and grabbed my handbag.

"I'm going to give him a quick call," I said.

I dashed between the tables debating whether I could get away with a text message or if I should suck it up and call him. I mean, really, how awful was it that I'd forgotten our date? Liam was entitled to be hurt, or even angry, and I wasn't all that anxious to face the consequences of my actions—which was bad of me, I know.

But I'm not big on suspense. I decided this was a phone-call-worthy screw-up, and if Liam was upset, well, I deserved to hear about it.

Outside the bar I headed down the main corridor and paused near the exhibit hall entrance. Not a lot of people were around. I pulled out my phone and tapped Liam's name on my contact list, and paced aimlessly until his voicemail picked up.

I launched into an explanation that I'd had to leave on business unexpectedly and that I was sorry I had to cancel our date.

I saw no reason to mention that I'd known about it since early this morning.

As a way to boost my apology, I said I was sorry yet again and ended the call. Then I dashed off a text message with one more apology and even included an emoji sad face and a heart—which proves … well, something. I don't know what.

But no way could I figure it out at that moment because Jack Bishop was in the hallway, headed toward me.

CHAPTER FOUR

Jack strode through the hallway toward me looking awesome in a charcoal gray Tom Ford suit, white shirt, and conservative blue necktie. But he wasn't just a handsome face and a gorgeous body. He was the kind of guy who could handle anything—anything. Nothing threw him. He possessed a solid core of confidence and strength, and radiated an everything-will-be-okay vibe.

This was the first time I ever saw a crack in that look.

Jack stopped in front of me. "What did you see out there?"

No "hi", no "hello," no clever comment. Yeah, Jack was majorly stressed, all right.

I'd hit the highlights when we'd been at the labyrinth. I understood his need to hear it all again.

I figured he'd already been grilled by the homicide detectives, the Severin security team, and the HPA staff who'd hired him to make sure nothing like this happened. Likely, he'd face them again in the coming days until the murder was solved.

"Kayla and I got to the labyrinth at our appointed time," I told him. "We waited our turn, then went in."

"Your turn?" Jack asked.

"The monitor—what's-her-name, Bliss—made us wait."

"She deliberately held you back?"

I nodded. Jack's frown deepened.

"Bliss said that everyone was afforded the solitude of time alone in the labyrinth," I explained.

At the time, it had made sense. Now I wondered if she'd held us back for another reason, a more sinister reason. I could see that Jack thought the same.

"Nobody was in the labyrinth when we went through," I said. "When we got to the exit I saw the victim on the ground. I spotted no one nearby, or in the wooded area, or on the path back to the conference center."

"Nobody?" Jack asked.

"Nobody," I said, and felt like I'd disappointed him, somehow. "Who was she? Did you find out?"

I wasn't sure how much info the homicide detectives on the scene had shared with Jack. They could be weird about that sort of thing.

"Elita Winston," Jack said. "She owned a bed and breakfast at Lake Arrowhead."

Lake Arrowhead was in the San Bernardino Mountains about three hours east of here. Lots of recreation, boating, camping, family activities. Lots of huge vacation homes along the shoreline owned by the wealthy anxious to get out of Los Angeles and into the fresh air.

"Gardening equipment was discovered nearby," Jack said. "Looks as if a shovel was the murder weapon."

An ugly picture formed in my mind of Elita Winston exiting the labyrinth, then being struck on the head. I tried to push the image away, but couldn't.

"Who was with her in the labyrinth?" I asked.

"According to the monitor, she went through alone."

Okay, that was kind of weird.

"So, what are the detectives thinking?" I asked.

Jack shrugged, as if the cops—or anybody—had only a best guess at the moment.

"There's speculation that someone followed her there, then waited until she went through the labyrinth and confronted her," he said. "An argument, maybe, that escalated."

"Or somebody was lying in wait for her at the exit," I said.

"How would the murderer have known when she'd go through?" Jack shook his head. "Risky."

"Not really," I said. "All the first-time attendees at the conference had priority through the labyrinth. There was a schedule. Everybody was assigned a departure time."

Jack sank deeper into thought. I could almost see his mind working, trying to fit the information together.

"What about Rosalind Russo?" I asked. "Have the detectives talked to her?"

Jack's gaze came up quickly. I got a little thrill that, obviously, he hadn't learned about her yet.

"She just won a cooking competition on television," I explained. "The Comfort Food Championship. It was a pretty big deal."

"What's she doing here?" Jack asked.

"Beats me," I said. "I saw her with the victim earlier."

Kayla had reminded me that I'd seen them briefly when we were with Shannon looking at the messenger bag on display in the exhibit hall. The image of Rosalind and Elita played through my mind. Elita, dressed in a designer business suit—red, to get noticed, and accessorizes right off a Neiman Marcus mannequin— and Rosalind in a mouse-brown dress and flats. Rosalind hadn't seemed to be enjoying the meet-and-greet as much as Elita.

"Elita was introducing her to everybody," I said. "Kind of showing her off."

"I'll check it out," Jack said.

He paused, looked away, then turned to me again and eased closer.

"This situation … it could …." Jack shook his head. I knew what he was thinking. This situation could sink his business permanently.

"I need your help, Haley."

"I'm on it."

Jack nodded. "Thanks," he whispered, and walked away.

I watched him go, my mind screaming with things I could do to solve Elita Winston's murder. My cell phone rang, jarring me, yanking me back into the moment.

Pulling it out of my handbag, it flew into my head that it was my ex-official boyfriend Ty calling, wanting to talk—which I was definitely not up for.

Then I felt guilty because my first thought hadn't been that Liam, my current official boyfriend, was calling me back about our date I'd just cancelled.

Honestly, I wasn't all that anxious to talk to either of them—and it had nothing to do with watching Jack as he walked away. Nothing. I swear.

I glanced at my phone. My mom's name blazed on the screen.

Crap.

I let the phone ring, debating whether to answer—which was bad of me, I know. But my mom and I—well, to be generous, I'll just say that we don't always click. She's a former beauty pageant queen, something I have no interest in or ability for. Yet, as obvious as that was from the time I took my first steps, it didn't stop her from putting me into every conceivable type of class trying to dig out a kernel of actual talent in me. It wasn't pretty. Nor enjoyable.

Still, Mom was Mom. I answered her call.

"Trousdale or Beverly Hills?" she asked.

I had no idea what she was talking about. Often, she didn't either—or so it seemed to me.

"And, of course, there's Brentwood," Mom went on. "But Brentwood is so … something. I don't know. Something. Don't you think?"

I didn't bother to respond.

"Maybe downtown, one of those gorgeous new high-rise developments," Mom said. "*Going up* is the thing now."

A faint idea of what she was talking about sparked in my head.

"It's near the Beverly Center," she said. "So convenient."

I froze.

"Of course, there's always Hancock Park," Mom said.

"Mom, are you talking about selling the house and moving?" I asked, panic rising in me.

"I told you all about it," she said.

"No, you didn't."

She didn't answer, her thoughts elsewhere—on something important to *her*, I'm sure.

"You're selling our house?" I said that kind of loud. The few people in the hallway nearby turned and stared. "Our home? You're selling our *home*?"

Home was a small mansion in the hills of La Cañada Flintridge, a gorgeous community near Pasadena that overlooked the Los Angeles basin. Mom had inherited it decades ago, along with a trust fund, from some long-dead relative. We'd always lived there. I had no memories of living anywhere else. And Mom wanted to sell it?

A glimmer of hope flared in my head.

"Does Dad know about this?" I asked.

"Yes, of course he knows."

"And he agreed to it?"

She was quiet for a moment. "Maybe somewhere along Wilshire."

With Mom, I often had to struggle to keep a conversation focused. I think it had something to do with her years on the pageant circuit. For her, staying on point ranked far below walking gracefully in five inch pumps, answering if-I-were-a-color-which-one-would-I-be questions on the fly, and recognizing the subtle difference between ecru and eggshell accessories.

Mom often ran off half-crazed with some new idea that she soon forgot about. Usually, I let it go and whatever it was eventually played out.

No way could I let this go and merely hope for the best.

"Mom? Is Dad okay with selling the house?"

My dad was an aerospace engineer, the sensible one in the marriage.

"Well, yes, of course," Mom said.

She blabbed on but I stopped listening.

Oh my God. *Oh my God.* My parents were selling our home—actually selling it.

I paced through the corridor, seeing nothing, hearing nothing, trying to get some perspective. My brother and I had moved out, and my sister, still in college and often away on modeling assignments, was hardly ever there. So, yeah, I guess Mom and Dad were free to sell, to move, to start over someplace else.

But, jeez, to sell, move, start over someplace else? Just like that?

"So you'll get back to me on this?" Mom asked, jarring me into reality.

She didn't wait for my response, which was just as well because I had no clue what she was talking about.

"Let me know," she said, and ended the call.

She claimed Dad knew and was on board, but what about my brother and sister? Had they been told? Were they okay with it?

I dashed off a text message to both of them.

I stood there in the hallway, all sorts of thoughts and memories battering my brain. Mom's news had shaken me up like a snow globe. I couldn't seem to process it.

So what could I do but think about murder instead?

As I headed down the hallway toward the bar where I'd left Kayla, I did an internet search on my phone. Jack had told me Elita Winston owned a B&B in Lake Arrowhead, so I figured that was a good place to start.

I found her site quickly and—wow—it looked like an awesome house. Situated along the shoreline, it was a big, two-story home with an A-frame roof and lots of balconies and porches overlooking the lake. There was a gazebo set among lush landscaping for weddings and other outdoor events. A path led to a dock and boat house.

The interior photos showed several rooms thoughtfully decorated, arranged as if each item had been selected with love and care for a specific spot, giving the home an appealing combo of rustic charm and casual elegance that was hard to pull off. No doubt about it, Elita Winston had excellent taste.

Elita's photo was there, too. She wore an awesome Michael Kors business suit. Her hair, nails, and makeup were done to perfection and her accessories were on point, a look hard to pull off without the help of a professional stylist. It made me kind of sad to see her.

The B&B was taking reservations for its upcoming grand opening, I saw as I clicked through the site. Elita must have been super confident that everything would be ready and would open on schedule. The reputation of what had to be an expensive endeavor was on the line. No way would she want to announce the opening, take reservations, then have to pull back on everything. What a public relations nightmare that would be. Word would spread that she was unreliable, and nobody—nobody—would risk booking an event with her.

I clicked another tab and saw Rosalind Russo's photo and the announcement that she was the B&B's chef, which surprised me. Rosalind was pictured standing in a kitchen, wearing an apron, and smiling the same modest smile I'd seen on the clip when she'd won the competition. The Comfort Food Championship logo was on the page.

I guess that explained why Elita had been introducing her around the conference earlier. Elita, it seemed, had jumped on Rosalind's win and newfound celebrity. No doubt Rosalind would be a great draw for the B&B. But I wondered why, of all the opportunities winning the competition would bring her way, Rosalind had agreed to be a chef at Elita's B&B, all the way out in Lake Arrowhead.

A zillion other questions flooded my brain, not the least of which was what would happen to the B&B now that Elita was dead. Would it become just another dream that never came to fruition? Did she have family or partners who would take over? Where would that leave Rosalind? And could anyone live up to the high standards Elita apparently had set for her business?

From everything I'd learned so far, Elita was smart, organized, competent, and capable. She must have been business savvy if she'd gotten an invitation to HPA ahead of her grand opening. The B&B she'd fashioned looked awesome and appeared to have a great future.

So who had wanted her dead?

And why?

CHAPTER FIVE

When I got back to the bar, Kayla was still seated at our table, still drinking wine.

"Nobody seems to know anything," she said and gestured to the people around us as I sat down. "I haven't overheard a word."

Kayla had excellent eavesdropping skills perfected in the breakroom and hallways at L.A. Affairs, and shared each juicy, gossipy word with little or no prompting, making her everything I ever wanted in a friend.

"Some grumbling about the labyrinth walk closing," she said, draining her glass. "I say, good for them for missing it, even if they didn't stumble over a dead body."

The server appeared. I needed to keep a clear head, but sitting here without a drink in front of me was a bar-foul I couldn't commit. We both ordered another wine.

"Has Shannon come by yet?" I asked.

"Nope." Kayla shook her head. "Maybe she's too upset. Maybe she quit. Maybe she couldn't deal with it."

Shannon had seemed competent and capable when she'd met us upon our arrival, but she did get kind of rattled when that whole thing about the swag in the messenger bags came up. It was anybody's guess how she was taking the news about the murder.

"No sign of the police, either," Kayla said. She squeezed her eyes shut for a few seconds, and frowned. "Oh my God. I don't want to talk to them. I don't want to get any more involved than I am. This whole thing has got me mega stressed."

"Give it until tomorrow," I suggested. "Things will look better in the morning."

Really, that made no sense, but everybody always said it. My emotional-support skills weren't the best so I had to go with whatever seemed to work for other people.

Kayla drew in a long breath and let it out slowly. "Yeah, I guess. As long as nothing else bad happens, as long as I don't have to get involved with it, or hear about it, or deal with it, or … anything."

This didn't seem like a good time to mention that I'd promised to help Jack find the murderer.

The server dropped off our wine. Kayla grabbed her glass and took a gulp, then squinted across the room.

"Oh my God," she whispered, and set her glass down. "I've got to lay off this stuff. I'm seeing things."

I turned and saw Mindy, the receptionist at L.A. Affairs, making her way toward our table. What the heck was she doing here?

"There you are. I've been looking all over for you," she moaned and dropped into a chair at our table.

I put Mindy in her forties, a plus-size gal with blonde hair shaped like a mushroom. She'd been our receptionist for a while—too long, really. I think it was a pity hire, which I would be okay with if she could manage the job. She was forever forgetting which clients came into the office, which interview room she'd put them in, who they wanted to see, and why they were there.

Mindy looked at me. "So, Hannah, where have you been all day?"

Yeah, and she always got everybody's name mixed up.

"It's Haley."

Mindy shook her head and sighed heavily. "Oh, dear. What a day I've had."

She looked exhausted, stressed, and frazzled—more so than usual.

"How about some wine?" Kayla asked.

"No, thank you, Karen," she said.

"Kayla," I told her.

"You're sure?" Kayla asked her. "One glass?"

Mindy sighed again. "I don't drink socially. It's mostly work-related."

"What are you doing here?" I asked. It came out sounding kind of harsh. But, jeez, come on. Priscilla was losing her mind, worried about L.A. Affairs' reputation, and she'd sent Mindy— *Mindy*—to the conference? I didn't get it.

"I'm taking care of our booths in the exhibit hall," Mindy said. "Handing out our brochures, smiling, being pleasant. You know, that sort of thing."

I hoped *that sort of thing* didn't include answering questions about our services.

"Everybody is supposed to be nice in the exhibit hall." Mindy eyed our wine. "They're not. Not everybody."

Kayla and I both sensed major gossip going down, so we leaned forward.

"People aren't being nice to you? That's awful," Kayla said. "What's happening?"

I was glad she spoke first. She sounded way more pleasant than I would have. Sure, I wasn't a big Mindy fan, but no way did I want somebody treating her badly.

"Well … Edith has the booth right next to ours—right next to us—and I know she saw me, but she acted like she didn't even know me. Of course, we haven't seen each other in a while. Not since she got married. A year or so ago, I think it was. She married *up*, obviously, though why she didn't take her new husband's name I don't know." Mindy's gaze drifted to our wine again. "Well … I guess one glass would be all right, since we're discussing work."

Kayla waved the server over and Mindy ordered a drink, which seemed to be just the reason she needed to keep talking.

"And it wasn't just me she wasn't being nice to," Mindy went on. "The way she spoke to Olivia. Terrible, just terrible. For a minute, I thought they might come to blows."

I accessed the conference info on my phone. Olivia Trent, I read—and was somewhat amazed that Mindy had gotten the name right—was the hostess supervisor. Maybe Olivia's problems with this Edith person explained why she hadn't showed up to smooth things over with Kayla and me, since Shannon hadn't appeared.

"Move this, add that. Do it *now*," Mindy went on. "All of a sudden, Edith had to do a demo. Video. Audio. Music. Wanted it added to her booth. Just like that."

Since I'd spent many months planning and executing all sort of events for L.A. Affairs' rich and famous clients, I knew what it was like to deal with a difficult customer, to shuffle things around at the last minute—and be pleasant while doing it. Not easy—and not the kind of client I'd want to work with again.

"Who is Edith?" I asked. "What kind of company does she have?"

The server brought Mindy's wine. She took a gulp and nodded graciously at Kayla. "This is delicious. You were right, Krystal."

"It's Kayla," I told her.

"Obviously, Edna is doing very well—"

"You mean Edith?" I asked.

"Yes, of course, that's what I said," Mindy said.

"You said *Edna,*" I pointed out.

"Maybe I did. Sometimes I do that," Mindy said, and touched her finger to her forehead. "I suffered a slight brain injury."

"Oh my God, that's awful," Kayla said. "What happened?"

"I don't remember," Mindy said. "Anyway, Edith is doing very well, she and her new husband. I saw the photos. He must have selected everything himself because, frankly, Edith's taste level is questionable. And good taste matters, especially at a bed and breakfast."

I got a weird feeling.

"She owns a B&B?" I asked.

"Oh, yes, up in the mountains," Mindy said. "Lake Arrowhead which, as you know, isn't cheap. He must be loaded."

Kayla and I exchanged a troubled look.

"Her name is Edith?" I asked. "You're sure?"

"Of course," Mindy said.

A this-has-be-a-clue-not-an-incredible-coincidence thought zapped my brain.

"Are you sure her name's not *Elita*?"

"I'm sure," Mindy said, taking another drink.

Damn. So much for uncovering a totally awesome clue.

"Her name is Edith," Mindy insisted. "We traveled in the same social circle for a while, back when I was married. I'm positive that's her name."

"Okay," I said.

Mindy uttered a faint grunt. "Now she's decided her name is Elita."

I nearly sprang out of my chair.

"You saw Elita Winston? Today? At her booth? Arguing with Olivia Trent?" I asked.

Mindy sipped and nodded. "Olivia was forced to give in, but I could tell it caused her all kinds of problems and she didn't like it. And who can blame her?"

Oh my God, that meant Mindy could have been one of the last people to see Elita alive.

A dreamy smile came over Mindy's face. "That chef who won the cooking challenge. I saw her, too. Right there at Edith's booth. It was so exciting. I'd watched the challenge on television. Every episode. Didn't miss a single one. I love those shows. I'm quite a good cook, if I say so myself."

"Rosalind was there, too, at Elita's booth, while this problem was going on?" I asked, just to make sure.

"She looked so embarrassed with Edith carrying on the way she was. I felt sorry for her. I guess she just couldn't take it any longer because suddenly, she disappeared." Mindy drained her glass. "I'm not looking forward to working our booth tomorrow, if Edith—Elita, whatever—is going to be there and make another scene."

"I don't think you have anything to worry about," I said.

We finished our drinks and talked about having dinner, but nobody was up for it. Mindy left, Kayla got a phone call, so I headed outside, thinking some fresh air would be good.

Standing at the front of the conference center I saw the blaze of high-powered lights at the labyrinth. The police and crime scene techs were still working. A helicopter swept low overhead and descended onto the helipad. I wondered if it was here as part of the investigation or if someone was making a grand entrance.

No way did I want to go near the labyrinth and everything that was going on there, so I headed in the opposite direction. A sidewalk took me away from the conference center and into a garden lit with twinkle and accent lights. A few other people were there, strolling, talking in low voices.

Spread out below me in the distance were the lights of Santa Barbara, stretching all the way to the dark expanse of the ocean. I drew in a couple of deep breaths, trying to shake off the anxiety of the day, trying to clear my thoughts. It didn't help. Elita Winston's murder was front and center in my mind.

Mindy hadn't heard Elita was dead. Apparently, the conference center was keeping it quiet and, possibly, had no intention of announcing it. Their PR department was, no doubt, working overtime to deal with the news. I wondered what reason they would give for Elita's absence—if they addressed it at all.

That made me think about Olivia Trent. As the hostess supervisor, she wouldn't have stepped into the situation with Elita's demands for changes to her booth unless the assigned hostess had been unable to deal with the last minute, somewhat outrageous, additions Elita wanted. When that sort of thing happened, it often escalated the problem rather than eased it.

One thing was certain—no matter how difficult Elita had been, the whole incident would have looked bad to everyone up the Severin supervision chain. The equipment, and the time and manpower needed to install it, cut into the conference profit. And, of course, it looked bad that nobody had anticipated the requests and prepared for them. Also, according to Mindy, the situation had risen into a full-on confrontation, something that could blow back on Olivia for not effectively dealing with an unhappy client.

I strolled along the walkway, imagining myself in Olivia's position. There would be explanations she'd have to give. Her competence might be called into question. Maybe her job would be on the line.

All because of Elita.

And now Elita had been murdered.

I wondered, too, what had prompted the changes to the booth. Mindy had said Elita wanted audio and video installed for a demonstration. Did she intend to showcase Rosalind's culinary skills? Elita had treated her like a show pony, so it made sense that she'd push Rosalind's celebrity as far as she could to publicize her B&B.

But was Elita behind the changes? Or was it Rosalind?

Maybe Rosalind had insisted on the demo. Maybe she felt entitled, after winning the nationally televised cooking championship. Maybe the modest, timid smiles I'd seen on her face were calculated, fake, a way to make herself look humble and, therefore, sympathetic and deserving.

Really, I had no way of knowing, at this point.

I needed to find out more about Rosalind and Olivia. I'd get on that first thing tomorrow. A warm glow ignited in my chest thinking that now I had two suspects I could tell Jack about.

My phone chimed. I dug it out of my handbag and saw that I had a message from Priscilla, wanting an update. I was tempted to ask her why the heck she'd sent Mindy here to represent L.A. Affairs, but decided to let it go for now. I also wanted to know who Priscilla had assigned to handle my events while I was here, but decided that, too, could wait until tomorrow.

Really, there's only so much I can handle at once.

I tapped an enthusiastic message to Priscilla—sprinkled liberally with emojis, which proved everything was great—and sent it. As I was tucking my phone away, it chimed again, signaling another text message.

The image of Ty flew into my head. He'd been okay with me needing time to think things over, but he wouldn't wait for long. Had his patience run out?

Then Mom appeared in my thoughts. Was she wanting my response to whatever the heck she'd asked me about earlier?

I braced myself and looked at my phone. Liam's name appeared.

Jeez, why do I always think of him last?

His text said he missed me, but understood my work situation. It was sprinkled liberally with emoji's—which proved everything was great. Right?

I tucked my phone away and headed back toward the conference center. Lights still blazed at the crime scene. The helicopter lifted off.

I thought about Jack. I wondered how he was holding up. I wondered if he'd made any progress on the investigation.

I wondered where he was sleeping tonight.

CHAPTER SIX

Kayla claimed she never ate breakfast—her way of not admitting she had a hangover, which I was totally onboard with since I'd made the same claim a time or two myself—so I left her in the room we shared and headed for the conference area. I'd selected a totally awesome gray suit with a do-I-know-how-to-accessorize-or-what Coach satchel, and felt pretty darn good.

The suit and pumps were just the excuse I needed to blow off the conference's recommended morning bird walk—I mean, really, a bird walk?—but since Priscilla was tracking our every movement as if we were a parolees with ankle bracelets, I stepped outside and snapped a selfie in front of some bushes. I sent it to her along with a glowing report on all the birds I'd seen, complete with lots of hey-this-thing-is-great emojis.

As I crossed the lobby and walked down the main corridor, I saw that the double doors to the exhibit hall were still closed. I spotted a breakfast station set up nearby, manned by a Severin employee doling out coffee and pastries. Several conference attendees clustered around it while others chatted and worked their phones.

Coffee and pastries—really, caffeine and sugar. Just the boost my morning needed. The only way it could have been better was if I were at a Starbucks—the best place on the planet—having my favorite drink in the entire universe, the mocha frappuccino.

I headed for the breakfast station then froze when I spotted something even more delectable—Jack Bishop. My heart rate picked up a little.

Oh my God, he looked fabulous. He had on a dark suit and conservative necktie, and was standing with two hot looking guys, both of whom were tall and muscular—as if all they did was workout and eat kale—and were totally handsome dressed in great suits. Though I didn't know them personally, I was positive they worked for Jack. They were just the sort of security guys he employed.

Jeez, if only I could get him to let me assist with the hiring—of course, there'd be the problem of how many tissues I'd go through with all the drooling I'd be doing. I was positive I could push through.

Jack finished his conversation and the two guys moved away. He spotted me and walked over.

I really wished I could do a slow motion hair flip right now.

"Anything new?" I asked.

Up close, I could see the tight lines around his eyes and mouth, the worry etched in his brow. I wasn't used to seeing Jack this way. I didn't like it. It made me worry, too.

He glanced around and moved closer. Wow, he smelled great.

"The detectives reviewed the surveillance tape," he said in a low voice. "There's no coverage at the labyrinth walk, so nothing helpful there. The gardeners admitted they left their equipment near the crime scene, but said it wasn't unusual since it's out of sight of the guests. Severin management confirmed it."

Jack hadn't held back the info—which was unusual for him, and told me how desperate he was for any help I could give him. It also meant the cops were still looping Jack in on developments, a good sign.

"So the detectives are thinking the murderer knew the equipment would be there?" I asked. "An employee?"

He shrugged. "Or anybody who'd walked the grounds, looking for a place and method to murder somebody."

"Still, likely an employee," I said. "The area near the labyrinth exit is rugged, compared to the rest of the grounds. A guest wouldn't likely go there."

"Maybe," he said. "I got some background on the victim. Married. Grown kids. No criminal activity. No red flags, so far."

I thought about telling Jack what Mindy had mentioned in the bar yesterday about how Elita had re-married and hadn't changed her name, but didn't see how it fit into the murder investigation. Besides, I knew his office staff would find out on their own.

"There was a confrontation between Elita and the hostess supervisor yesterday," I said. "It got ugly."

Jack's brows rose, telling me he hadn't heard this.

"Her name is Olivia Trent. I'm going to talk to her today," I said. "Have the detectives spoken with Rosalind Russo?"

His lip twitched. "They haven't made that connection yet."

I took that to mean Jack hadn't passed along the info on Rosalind that I'd given him yesterday. I didn't blame him for not sharing. He'd want—need—to solve this murder himself, if he had any hope of salvaging the reputation of his business. I knew, too, that the homicide detectives would find their way to Rosalind, sooner rather than later, which meant Jack had to solve it fast.

"I'll let you know what I find out," I said.

Jack nodded and left.

Kayla and I were expected to attend one of the workshops this morning. No way could I face a kill-me-when-I-doze-off presentation without a brain boost. I grabbed a doughnut and coffee—thank God there was French vanilla creamer—at the breakfast station and settled at one of the tall tables nearby.

The crowd in the main corridor had picked up, and surged forward when a Severin employee unlocked the doors to the exhibit hall. Immediately, my gaze locked onto the Titan messenger bag on display.

Sure, Jack had a much bigger problem on his hands, but I wondered who—if anyone—was looking for the stolen bags. The theft was a huge deal. Four bags, costing thousands of dollars. They'd have to be replaced, along with the donated swag, before the giveaway at the end of the conference—no way to back out now, with the display bag prominently featured for everyone to see and drool over.

Who was liable for the loss? The HPA conference? Severin? Jack? Somebody was going to have to shell out major bucks to make this right—and deal with the blow back to everyone's reputation if word got out about the theft.

And what about the swag inside each of the stolen bags? If anyone came forward trying to use one of the vouchers, would it be honored? Or would they be accused of receiving stolen merchandise and face a police investigation?

I sipped my coffee and finished my doughnut. Yeah, okay, the bags were totally hot, raging-fantastic. But who would want four—I mean, really, *four*—of them? What could be done with them? Sell them, or maybe give them as gifts. So that meant the thief could be a Casale lover, or a plain old criminal looking to move the bags for a quick profit—both of which would make recovering them almost impossible.

Not great news for Jack's reputation.

I checked the time on my phone—no text from Priscilla, thank God—and saw that the first workshop would begin shortly. I could have sat there and had more coffee or another doughnut— tempting, yes—or I could have gotten a jump on the day's activities, reviewed the conference schedule, planned all the things I could do to promote L.A. Affairs and enhance our reputation among the conference attendees—the thing Kayla and I had been sent here for.

No way. Not when Jack needed my help to solve a murder, and outrageously fabulous Titan messenger bags had to be recovered.

I dumped my trash and headed into the exhibit hall. Rows of vendor booths wound around the huge room. There was a low rumble of conversations as people moved through the aisles.

After getting momentarily distracted by the Titan messenger bag on display—and noticing the swag donation brochures had been removed—I moved along with the crowd. Right away I spotted Mindy manning the L.A. Affairs booth.

Our booth looked good, stocked with brochures, business cards, and photos of some of the extravagant events L.A. Affairs had staged. I recognized several of the parties I'd handled. Cool.

"Would you like a brochure?" Mindy asked, holding one out.

Good grief.

"It's me," I said. "Haley."

Mindy frowned.

"I work here," I added.

"Oh, yes. Of course, Hannah."

"Haley," I told her. She didn't seem to hear me so I pushed on. "How's it going?"

Honestly, I wasn't all that interested in how much traffic our booth was getting, and yeah, sure, that sounded kind of bad of me. What I wanted was to catch Rosalind here and, hopefully, Olivia, too, so I could talk to them and either mark them off of my I-think-you-did-it suspect list, or get them to whoo-hoo-look-at-me-go confess. I needed to find them quickly. I didn't have *forever* to solve Elita's murder.

"Everybody is so friendly, and is saying such nice things about us. Our brochures are going fast. I had to re-order already." Mindy's smile vanished as she nodded toward the booth next to ours. "All's quiet over there, thank goodness."

No one was manning Elita's booth and no brochures were on display. Prominently positioned was Rosalind's photo featuring the Comfort Food Championship logo. No mention of a scheduled cooking demo.

"Has Rosalind been here yet?" I asked.

Mindy ignored my question, or wasn't paying attention, or wasn't listening. I don't know which. I never know what's going on with her.

"I'm surprised Edith—or Elita, or whatever—isn't here yet," Mindy said, still eyeing the B&B booth.

Obviously, Mindy still hadn't learned that Elita was dead. I had heard no official announcement from the conference. Apparently, as I suspected, they were going to keep a lid on the whole thing.

"I hope Rosalind gets here soon," Mindy said, and sighed. "I can't wait to see her cooking demonstration."

I couldn't wait to ask her if she had an alibi for Elita's murder.

"What about Olivia?" I asked. "Has she been by yet?"

"Oh, Zander, that was quick," Mindy said, doing a little finger wave at somebody behind me.

Again, she ignored my question. Good thing I was so self-confident. I could get a complex.

A guy in a Severin polo shirt, pushing a cart loaded with boxes, stopped at the booth. He was blonde, maybe a college student, kind of hot looking. I recognized him from yesterday at the Titan messenger bag display when he'd delivered brochures there.

He flashed a big smile. "I'm here to serve," he said, and started unloading L.A. Affair tri-folds from one of the boxes.

"Zander keeps all the booths stocked," Mindy said to me. "I don't have to go to the stockroom for anything. In fact, none of the vendors bother going back there."

At the word *stockroom*, visions of the other portion of my life popped into my head. Despite my oh-so fabulous position at L.A. Affairs, I still had my part-time job at Holt's Department Store— long story. While I did a bang-up job as an event planner, I'd put my own spin on my sales clerk duties, which included hiding out from customers in the store's stockroom.

The image of my ex-official boyfriend Ty flamed in my head, along with the things that had happened with him in the Holt's stockroom. Nothing naughty, just … well, anyway, I couldn't think about that now. Ty had given me the shock of my life a few days ago when he'd showed up at my apartment. I'd dodged a response but … well, I couldn't think about that now, either.

"Thank you, Zander," Mindy said, bringing me back to the moment.

"Let me know when you need anything else. I'm just a text message away." Zander nodded to Elita's booth. "I'm sure I'll be back as soon as *she* gets here."

He moved on and I decided I should do the same.

The crowd was starting to thin out as I walked through the aisles. I pretended to look at the exhibits—most of them looked totally awesome, and not one of them seemed like the kind of company you'd find in your spam folder—but I was really trying to spot Rosalind or Olivia. My cell phone chirped so I grabbed it from my handbag and saw a text from Kayla telling me to meet her at the workshop we were supposed to attend.

Okay, having to do actual conference functions while at the conference was really annoying, but I didn't have a choice. Then, thankfully, as I was headed for the door I spotted Olivia Trent.

I recognized her from her photo on the Severin website. I put her at mid-thirties, average height and build, with brown hair pulled back in a no-nonsense low ponytail. She was talking with a guy at one of the vendor booths, smiling and nodding, looking as if her morning was off to a great start.

I was about to make her day.

When she moved away from the booth, I stepped up and blocked her path. Olivia drew back, startled.

"Oh, yes, hello," she said, marshalling her required Severin I'm-always-pleasant smile. "Can I help you …?"

"Haley Randolph. L.A. Affairs," I told her, and didn't sound the least bit Severin-like. "I'm very disappointed in your conference."

Okay, I could have come out of the gate with a nicer comment, but I figured I'd put her on the defensive immediately, and in her desperation to smooth things over with me I could catch her off guard with my questions about Elita's murder.

That's how all we super-cool sort-of private investigators roll.

Olivia drew herself up straighter and presented me with her I-can-fix-this expression.

"What seems to be the trouble?" she asked.

"I found a dead body here."

Her I-can-fix-this expression vanished quicker than a Betsy Johnson handbag on a Macy's after-Christmas sale table.

"And no one, not one single person from Severin, has spoken with us," I told her.

She opened her mouth to say something, but I didn't give her a chance. Thanks to having witnessed my beauty queen mom's I'm-better-than-you attitude with which she'd plowed through entire management chains from receptionist to corporate president, I knew I had this.

"Kayla, L.A. Affairs' other representative here, is completely distraught. I'm not sure she'll be able to continue with the conference," I told her.

Kayla could, of course, as long as the wine held out.

"Frankly, I'm appalled by the indifference that has been shown to Kayla and me," I said. "I expected Severin to have higher standards."

I kept going, figuring I was rolling pretty good.

"As you know, this is our first experience at HPA. So far, I've been able to keep the news from my management team at L.A. Affairs." I executed one of my mom's haughty eyebrow bobs, a favorite of hers. "But after the lack of concern from everyone here at Severin, I'm not sure why I should continue to do so."

"Shannon hasn't spoken to you?" Olivia asked, and looked genuinely surprised.

"She most certainly has not," I told her. "Where is she? Is she as upset by this horrific news as Kayla? Is she being ignored by Severin also?"

Yeah, okay, I was kind of stretching it there. But it seemed to work.

"No, of course not." Olivia shook her head, looking truly confused. "I specifically instructed Shannon to speak with you and Kayla, and offer any and all assistance you might need. I don't ... I don't understand what happened."

The thing about rolling over somebody was you had to know when to pull back.

I don't like pulling back.

Still, I could see that Olivia was on the ropes so no need to push any further.

"Obviously, this is a difficult time for everyone on staff," I said, as if we were both suddenly on the same side. "And you did instruct Shannon on how to handle the situation."

Olivia looked relieved that I had calmed down at little. "I'm sure there's a very good reason for Shannon's behavior. She's an excellent employee. Although she hasn't been with us long, she excelled at every facet of our training program, which is extensive and intense. I'm sure there's a very good reason she hasn't approached you or Kayla."

Now, of course, was the perfect moment to turn the conversation to something that would benefit *me*.

"I understand you had your hands full yesterday dealing with Elita Winston and her demands for changes," I said, like we were friends now.

"Nothing out of the ordinary," Olivia said, though she still seemed to be a bit lost in thought, probably wondering what was up with Shannon. "Dealing with clients is routine for me."

"Even clients who want their entire booth upgraded on a moment's notice?" I asked.

"Well, yes. That was a little unusual."

"More than unusual," I said. "A witness stated you two nearly came to blows."

Olivia's I-can-handle-anything posture crumbled. "What? Who said that?"

"Did you follow Elita to the labyrinth walk? Try to talk to her, smooth things over? And she refused to listen?" I asked. "Did things go too far?"

Her mouth flew open in an outraged gasp, then snapped shut. She squared her shoulders and said, "Please accept my apology on behalf of the Severin management team for not properly acknowledging and offering comfort for what you and Kayla experienced."

Olivia pushed past me and disappeared down the aisle.

She'd looked stunned and blind-sided by my accusation that she'd murdered Elita. She'd looked pretty convincing.

But she hadn't denied it.

CHAPTER SEVEN

Kayla waited outside the door to the workshop we were supposed to attend. I had to admit that, despite all the wine last night, she looked pretty darn good dressed in an awesome navy blue business suit, hair and makeup done.

"For Priscilla," she said, holding up her phone.

We posed in front of the sign that displayed the name of the workshop, and Kayla snapped a pic.

"Be sure to include lots of emoji," I said, as she tapped out a text message.

"Yeah, we're working hard," she mumbled.

We followed the flow of people into the room and I selected seats on the back row of the aisle closest to the door—my go-to spot for any sort of gathering that involved actually paying attention.

"What's the workshop about?" I asked.

Kayla swiped through her phone. "It's called *Creative Problem Solving.*"

Okay, so the first workshop of the conference was a bust for me. I had no problem solving my—or anyone else's—problems. I'm not bossy. I just know what everybody should do.

It's a gift, really.

The room filled up with well-dressed men and women, the speaker stepped up to the podium, and I drifted off.

During meetings my mind usually veered between any number of pleasant topics—my next shopping trip, getting together with friends, maybe seeing Liam soon—or simply making a mental grocery list. But, oddly enough, my first thought today was about my clients at L.A. Affairs.

I didn't have a lot of events in the planning stages, which wasn't unusual for this time of year since most everybody was still exhausted from the holidays. The next big moment on the let's-celebrate-this-even-though-nobody-really-knows-why calendar was Valentine's Day, otherwise known as Single Awareness Day.

I'd refused to take on any events for that day. Weeks ago when clients had contacted L.A. Affairs for help staging Valentine's events, I was still kind of stinging from my breakup with Ty and even though I was seeing Liam, we hadn't been official—well, we were kind of official, but not *official* official. So no way did I want to knock myself out planning a fabulous day-evening-weekend-whatever for some other couple.

All of which was kind of selfish of me, but oh well. I mean, really, I have to draw the line somewhere.

Yet I did have events going. Everything was up to date with them but I figured I'd have heard from Priscilla by now with the name of the planner who was monitoring them for me. This seemed like the perfect moment to find out—and, of course, kill some time until the workshop ended.

I dug my phone out of my handbag and dashed off a quick text to Priscilla—emojis included. Then it vibrated and I saw a response from my sister about the message I'd sent yesterday. She was in London on a modeling assignment blah, blah, blah, and was in total panic mode, blah, blah, blah, about Mom's sudden idea to sell our family home.

That made me think of my brother, so I checked my messages and, sure enough, he'd weighed in on the situation. The whole thing was news to him and he was weirded-out by it. He's a pilot in the Air Force, stationed in the Middle East, and almost never got upset about anything, which says a lot about how out-there Mom's news was.

Okay, so all three of us were onboard the how-can-she-do-this bandwagon. But what could we do about it? I reminded myself that all of this upset might be for nothing. Mom often got distracted, usually by looking at herself in the mirror, so maybe this whole thing would blow over.

Crossing my fingers and hoping for the best wasn't much of a plan, but it was the only thing I could come up with at the moment.

As I tucked my phone away, the noise level in the room amped up and everybody rose from their chair. Jeez, the workshop was over already?

"So what was this about?" I asked Kayla as we headed toward the door.

"Solving problems," she said. "Ways to energize and refocus your team."

I saw no need to energize or refocus my team—all they had to do was follow my instructions. Just as well the workshop had passed me by, unnoticed.

We moved along the hallway and I spotted Shannon positioned by the wall, stretching up, scanning the crowd. She saw me at the same instance and waved us over.

"Haley, Kayla, please accept my most sincere apology for not speaking with you yesterday about the … incident," Shannon said.

She looked genuinely sincere—actually, she genuinely looked like somebody who'd gotten majorly reprimanded by her supervisor for not following procedure.

"I know that was a horrific thing for you to witness," Shannon said. "I'm so sorry you had to endure it."

"It was pretty awful," Kayla told her.

"Yes, it was," Shannon agreed. "How are you two feeling today? Better?"

If anyone needed to feel better, it was Shannon. She didn't look so hot—pale, tense, grim, like she might be physically sick at any moment.

Olivia must have really lit into her—which I guess was kind of my fault, after the way I'd lit into Olivia about Elita's murder.

"Mostly, I'm just trying to forget about it," Kayla said.

My kind-of super-sleuthing instincts took over, so I said, "What's the latest on the murder investigation?"

Shannon's already pale face faded another shade. "I have no idea. Why would I? I'm not involved. I'm not involved in any sort of capacity."

Before I could ask anything else, Shannon said, "If you need anything, if there's anything I can do, please don't hesitate to let me know."

She hurried away.

"I think she's taking it harder than I am," Kayla muttered. She glanced at her phone. "The next workshop starts soon."

"What's this one?"

"*Re-invigorate and Transform Your Day*," she read.

While I'd been through a lot of days that I'd wished could be re-invigorated or transformed—like today, for instance—I wasn't all that crazy about sitting through a presentation about it. Especially when I had something way more important to do.

"I'll meet you there," I said, and headed down the hall.

I figured the best place to find Rosalind—my other she-probably-did-it murder suspect—was in the exhibit hall. Hopefully, she was hanging out at Elita's B&B booth. If not, I was sure Mindy was still on celeb-watch and I could get her to text me if Rosalind showed up.

A pretty good-sized crowd roamed the exhibit hall—jeez, why weren't these people in a workshop—and as I wormed my way through, I spotted Rosalind manning Elita's booth. That hot guy Zander was there, chatting her up.

"Excuse me, Zander. I could use a few more brochures," Mindy said, stepping from behind the L.A. Affairs booth. "Just tell me where to find them in the stockroom and I'll pick up what I need."

Zander pushed his cart in front of her, blocking her path.

"I'll get them," he said, flashing a smile.

"No, really," Mindy said. "The stockroom isn't far, and I don't mind. You've done too much already."

"Don't even think about it," he told her, smiling wider. "I'm here to make your day easier."

"Well, all right, if you're sure. If you really don't mind," Mindy said.

"I really don't mind," he told her.

Zander hit her with another display of his pearly-whites, and left.

She blushed slightly and turned to me. "Isn't he the sweetest thing? So helpful. What a nice young man."

"So Rosalind is here," I said, and nodded toward the B&B booth. "How's it going over there?"

"People have been stopping by, chatting. Some of them recognize her from the cooking championship," Mindy reported, them did prune-face. "So much better than yesterday when Elita was here."

"I'm pretty sure today will be quieter than yesterday," I told her, and walked over to the B&B booth.

"Hello, welcome." Rosalind uttered a self-conscious titter. "Thank you for stopping by."

She had on another ho-hum dress similar to the one I'd seen her in yesterday, flats, little makeup, with her hair in a this-is-really-the-best-I-can-manage up-do. She didn't come across as an I'll-gouge-your-eyes-out-to-win kind of gal so I figured I'd do better easing into the real reason I was here.

I introduced myself, then said, "You won the Comfort Food Championship on TV, right?"

"I did," she said, and dipped her lashes. "I was so lucky, so lucky."

"I think it was more than luck," I said. "You must be an excellent chef."

"Thank you," she murmured. "But I was lucky to be on the show at all. I didn't make the final round of auditions, so I thought I was just *out*. Then the production company called me at the last minute and said one of the contestants couldn't compete, so I was *in*."

"What happened with the other contestant?" I asked.

Rosalind glanced away. "Some sort of accident, or something. I don't really know."

"And now you're the chef at Elita's B&B?" I asked. "I figured the TV network would have given you your own show."

"Well, there's been some talk," she admitted, with a modest smile.

"So why are you at the B&B?" I asked, and managed a genuinely puzzled expression.

Her smile dimmed slightly. "I accepted the job with Elita before the network called to tell me I could be in the competition after all. Elita and I were friends. I couldn't back out."

"But if you were friends, it seems like she'd have wanted you to be available for your own TV show," I said, and pulled off an I'm-kind-of-confused tone pretty darn well.

"There were some ... legal ... issues."

Meaning Elita had her sign a contract, I figured. It was a serious move, considering Elita was supposedly her friend.

"So, anyway," Rosalind said, plastering on a bright smile, "the most exciting part of winning the championship was that I didn't know I'd won until the day the show aired, and the producer called and told me. All four of us finalists were filmed as if we'd won, so nobody could leak the info and spoil the show's finale."

"That's really awesome," I said. "Too bad you can't take advantage of all the publicity and opportunities because you're stuck in a B&B in Lake Arrowhead."

"Well ... that might change," Rosalind said, and shifted uncomfortably.

"I know about Elita," I told her.

Her gaze came up sharply. "What ... what do you mean?"

I leaned closer. "I know what happened to her."

Rosalind seemed to deflate. "Oh, it's terrible, just terrible. All this pretending. I don't understand. Everybody insisted I stay, man this booth, so nobody would suspect something had happened. At least I don't have to do the cooking demonstration Elita insisted on. But what am I supposed to say to people who stop by? I don't even have a brochure to hand out—Zander can't find them. And what am I supposed to do about Friday?"

She looked at me as if she expected me to have answers. I didn't, of course, so she kept talking.

"I don't like it here. I don't want to stay. I don't understand. Where's her family? Why aren't they here?"

Rosalind looked completely frazzled now—the best time for me to hit her with my suspicion.

"What happened at the labyrinth walk?" I asked.

Rosalind gasped and went white. "I have no idea."

"You weren't with her?" I asked. Jack had told me she wasn't, but I wanted to hear it from Rosalind herself.

"No. No, I was nowhere near that place."

"Why not? Why didn't you two go through together?" I asked. "I saw you earlier in the evening. Elita was talking to everyone about your win, showing you off. Why not at the labyrinth?"

"I—I didn't want to go. I—I didn't feel good. I was tired. My feet hurt. I don't like that sort of thing."

Rosalind soared past frazzled to frantic, and was closing in on losing it. I knew it was time to change tactics.

"Look, I'm just trying to help you out here," I said in my you-can-trust-me voice. "The police are going to question you, so—"

She plastered her hand over her mouth, barely suppressing a scream, and raced away.

I was about to go after her when Olivia Trent planted herself in front of me, a smug look leaking through her I'm-required-to-give-good-service expression.

"Excuse me," I said, and dodged around her.

She moved with me, blocking me.

"Homicide detectives are here," Olivia said, looking all together pleased with herself. "They want to question you in the murder of Elita Winston."

Oh, crap.

CHAPTER EIGHT

As homicide detectives go, those two were pretty lame—which benefited me in the best possible way. I'd spoken with them for a few minutes in a small conference room tucked away near the business center, and they'd asked routine questions. I'd provided routine answers—basically that I'd seen, heard, and witnessed nothing useful—and they'd sent me on my way with their thanks. I had a feeling they'd eventually talk to Kayla, which I was sure would freak her out big-time, but I figured she was down their list a ways thanks to my I-saw-nothing answers.

It was a relief, for once, to not be considered a suspect, to basically get a pass on the interview. I'd been tempted to ask the detectives for an update on the investigation—old habit—but I was afraid it would compromise my I'm-totally-clueless remarks. I did manage to sneak in an I'm-lost question about why somebody would want to murder the owner of a B&B. Honestly, the detectives had looked totally clueless, too, so I figured it was just as well I hadn't asked for specifics.

As I headed through the main corridor away from the business center, I spotted Jack. I'd texted him, asking to meet up. This meant I'd had to blow off the entire workshop—the name of which I'd forgotten—but it was a sacrifice I was willing to make. Besides, I knew Kayla could fill me in on it later.

Jack looked as handsome as always, in an awesome suit and necktie that set off the color of his eyes. He also looked even more stressed out than when I'd last seen him.

"Have you got something?" Jack asked.

Right to business. Yeah, he was stressed big-time.

I shifted into private-investigator-wanna-be mode, and told him I'd talked to Olivia, the one person I knew who'd had a confrontation with Elita and also had access to the exact time she was scheduled to walk through the labyrinth.

"She was stunned that I'd questioned her involvement," I said. "But she didn't deny anything."

Jack looked positively underwhelmed with my news. Understandable.

"I spoke to Rosalind, too." I gave him the rundown on how she'd been a last-minute contestant on the cooking championship show, and that by then she was under contract to Elita for her B&B.

"Seems to me Rosalind has more motive than anyone," I went on. "Elita was holding her back from what was probably the biggest opportunity of her life."

Jack nodded. "Anything else?"

"What's up with Elita's family?" I asked. "Have any of them showed up here?

"Her husband's an accountant. Some kind of health problem," Jack explained. "Still checking on him."

"What about her kids?" I asked.

"Stepkids," Jack said, and shook his head. "None of the family has been here."

I thought about how, after learning from Mom that she intended to sell the family home, I'd immediately contacted my brother and sister, and I'd heard back from them right away. It seemed odd to me that nobody from Elita's family had been here, talking to the detectives, the conference center management, and Jack, demanding answers.

"Does that seem weird to you?" I asked.

"Families ...," Jack mumbled and shrugged it off.

"I keep wondering who would murder a B&B owner, and why?" I said. "Did she have a partner in the business? A dispute with the locals in Lake Arrowhead? Other B&B owners in the area who weren't happy with more competition?"

"I got the report from the office a few minutes ago." Jack pulled out his phone, scanning as he swiped through the screens.

"Local merchants were glad to have another business going in. The property had been in the family for years. No squabbles with the neighbors. No problems with the construction crews refurbishing the house."

Huh. Not exactly any red hot clues there.

"Did you get anything useful from Rosalind?" Jack asked.

I didn't want to tell him that—again—I'd come up with basically nothing helpful, so I went with what little I knew.

"I definitely got a weird vibe from her about Elita's murder," I said. "It seems strange to me that Rosalind wasn't with Elita at the labyrinth walk. When I asked Rosalind about it, she was evasive."

Jack seemed unimpressed, but he kept listening.

"I guess they could have had a blow-up," I said. "Rosalind wasn't happy about the fuss Elita was causing over the impromptu cooking demo she wanted done in the exhibit hall. Add that to Elita screwing her over by insisting she keep to their agreement about working at the B&B, preventing her from the opportunity of a lifetime with that food show. Maybe what started out as a simple argument grew into something worse."

"Do you think Rosalind is capable of murder? Physically capable?"

Rosalind was kind of soft around the middle and she wasn't very tall. But surely she'd worked up some good arm muscles with all that stirring, whipping, and lifting she'd been doing in the kitchen. Swinging that shovel at Elita's head with enough force to kill her wouldn't have been hard.

"I think she is," I said. "Plus, she has a heck of a motive."

We were both quiet for a moment, both thinking over the possibility. I wanted to ask Jack if he'd made progress on the theft of the messenger bags—yes, my brain had rushed ahead—but his phone chirped. He glanced at it, gave me an apologetic eyebrow bob, and took off.

The corridor was kind of empty because the workshop was still going on. No way did I want to go there and catch the end of the presentation. I'd already spoken with Olivia and Rosalind, my two suspects, and gotten nothing. Jack hadn't offered anything new. What the heck was I supposed to do now?

Then it hit me.

Oh, crap. Guess I'd have to do some real work.

I checked my phone and saw several text messages from Priscilla. Swiping past the ones asking for an update on the conference, I found the one she'd sent with the name of the planner who was taking care of my events while I was here.

Yikes! Nadine? Priscilla had assigned Nadine to look after my clients and events?

Okay, really, I didn't know Nadine very well—but that was no reason not to like her. I'd run into her a few times in the office breakroom and, of course, seen her in meetings. She was a few years younger than me, with auburn hair and green eyes, and dressed in fabulous clothes and accessories, as required by L.A. Affairs.

She'd started out in the cube farm, doing—well, I don't know exactly what they do there. Accounting, supply requisition, something. But she'd blasted her way up the ranks quickly and now, it seemed, Priscilla was giving her a shot at event planning by subbing for me.

Event planners made a higher salary than the gals in the cube farm, we got awesome perks, plus it was a more prestigious position, and—a personal favorite of mine—planners could leave the office whenever we wanted to, claiming it was to meet a client or a vendor.

From the rumors I'd heard about Nadine—I hadn't started any of them, but depending on how she managed my events, now I might have to—she was really aggressive, not at all particular about whose toes she stepped on, or overly concerned about the quality of her work.

No way did I want my events to be the office crash test dummies for an up-and-coming planner.

It occurred to me that maybe this was a compliment. Maybe Priscilla knew that all of my events were up-to-date and wouldn't need much monitoring while I was gone, and that's why she'd put a newbie in charge of them.

Compliment or not, it didn't sit well with me, but I decided I could give her a chance.

I called Nadine. She answered, and when I identified myself she immediately put me on hold.

"I just got off the phone with the Drakes," Nadine said, when she came back on the line. "I think I've got them settled down. Don't worry."

Don't worry? Why should I worry? Everything for their fortieth wedding anniversary party and their fifty guests was handled.

"Here's what I think should happen," Nadine went on. "Since they met in India all those years ago, I want them to enter the party riding elephants."

She wanted them to—what?

"It will be memorable," Nadine said.

"It will be irresponsible." I might have said that kind of loud. "The Drakes are seniors. Mrs. Drake just recovered from hip replacement surgery."

"My personal ethos is to think outside of the lines on these events," Nadine told me.

"It's an outrageous idea," I said. "Don't even mention this to the Drakes."

"I'll run it by Priscilla."

"No. Don't—"

Nadine hung up.

Crap.

Immediately, I wanted to reach through the phone and strangle Nadine. That wasn't possible, so I accessed my contacts list and tapped on Priscilla's number.

No way was I going to let Nadine hijack my carefully thought out and well-orchestrated events—especially for a fantastic couple like the Drakes. Priscilla's voicemail picked up. Tempted as I was to leave a scathing message—at the top of my lungs—I didn't think it would be in the best interest of my long-term employment to blast the office manager with her incompetent choice of replacement.

Call me crazy.

I hung up.

Still, I had to do something

I was tempted to send a text to Kayla, telling her about the situation. She was still in the workshop and I knew she'd leave immediately—my kind of friend. But if she left in the middle of it, how was she going to be able to tell me what it was about when Priscilla asked?

I decided to walk off some of my upset and found myself in the exhibit hall. I wandered through the aisles, pretending to look at the booths. At the back of the room I saw that hottie Zander coming out of a discreet hallway that I figured led to the stockroom, pushing a cart loaded with boxes of supplies for the vendors. He smiled when he saw me. The Severin training must be some heavy duty indoctrination. Zander seemed to be easily handling the endless job of fetching and carrying for the vendors by himself—I hadn't seen anyone but him working the hall—yet he always seemed happy to do so.

Weird, huh?

I kept walking and spotted Elita's B&B booth. No one was there. At the L.A. Affairs booth, Mindy stood at her post, talking with a man I'd never seen before.

I figured him for fiftyish, dressed in a well-cut though not terribly expensive suit. He had carefully groomed gray hair and a mustache inspired, no doubt, by Magnum P.I. cruising Oahu in Robin's Ferrari.

"Oh, here's one of our top planners now," Mindy announced as she gestured to me. "Come over, Hannah. Meet Charles."

"It's Haley," I said, politely, as I stopped next to the man. "And you're Charles? Really?"

He smiled. "Charles Kent. A pleasure to meet you, Haley."

Charles spoke with one of those kind-of British accents that made a person sound witty, charming, and knowledgeable, no matter what comment was made.

Maybe I should work on developing one of those.

"Charles owns a hotel chain," Mindy blurted out. Her cheeks were pink and her breathing was a little ragged. "A boutique chain catering to a highly exclusive clientele. Very successful."

"You're too kind, Mindy," he said and gave her a gracious grin.

Her cheeks grew redder.

"L.A. Affairs certainly got a choice spot for your booth," Charles said, glancing around. His expression clouded when his gaze landed on the B&B booth. "Though if it were me, I'd question the location, given recent events."

Charles's comment flew over Mindy's head, but it smacked me hard in the face.

"You heard about Elita?" I asked.

"From an acquaintance, not anyone affiliated with the conference," Charles said. "Frankly, I was surprised to see Elita here, but not surprised by what happened to her."

If I'd had this-could-be-a-smoking-hot-clue antenna, they would have sprouted out of my head and wiggled.

Just as I was formulating my I-need-more-dirt follow-up question, Mindy waved and announced, "Oh, look. Here's another one of our planners."

Kayla muscled between Charles and me, clutching her phone.

"We have to go, Haley," she told me, then lowered her voice. "It's Priscilla."

I glanced at her phone.

"We have to go," she said, her eyes bulging. *"Now."*

"Excuse us," I managed to say as I hurried after her.

"She just sent me another text," Kayla said, as we bobbed and weaved through the aisles and into the main corridor, now crowded with attendees. "About the live feed of the workshop."

There's a live feed?

"Priscilla saw it."

Priscilla could see it?

"She's not happy."

Oh, crap.

"She wants us both on a conference call," Kayla said. "Now."

I followed Kayla to a somewhat quiet corner of the main corridor, out of the flow of men and women, but before she could draw a breath, Rosalind broke out of the crowd and hurried over.

"I … I need to talk to you," Rosalind said.

Kayla gave her major stink-eye.

Rosalind leaned closer. "It's … it's about Elita's … you know."

Oh my God. Was Rosalind about the hit me with a major clue? A confession?

"Sure," I said. "Of course."

Kayla turned her stink-eye on me. I ignored her.

Rosalind stepped away and I followed. She wrung her hands and fidgeted. I glanced back at Kayla. She gestured to her phone and upped her stink-eye to mega stink-eye.

"I know you think I was involved with … with what happened to Elita," Rosalind said, barely above a whisper.

"Were you?" I asked.

"Well, actually …." Rosalind gulped. "I'm glad she's gone."

CHAPTER NINE

Kayla stomped over, waving her phone.

"I've got Priscilla," she hissed. "She's demanding to know why she didn't see us in the live feed from the workshop that just ended."

"The second workshop? Didn't you go?"

"I thought *you* were going," she said.

"I thought *you* were going.

Oh, crap.

"She claims she didn't see us," Kayla said. "She said we weren't asking questions, circulating through the room, networking, chatting up other vendors, talking up L.A. Affairs."

Okay, like I had time for this.

I had Rosalind standing two feet away, possibly ready to confess to murder. No way did I have time to deal with Priscilla over this morning's dumbass workshop.

Kayla was, understandably, bordering on total panic mode. Me, not at all. Dealing well with confrontation was one of the things I did best.

I thought of it as my superpower.

I channeled my beauty-queen mom's I'm-better-than-you attitude, which had helped me get out of many a tight spot in the past.

Hard to believe, but yes, occasionally Mom was helpful.

I grabbed Kayla's phone.

"Priscilla, I'm appalled you would question our participation in the workshop," I said, in my now-I'm-going-to-run-you-over voice.

She said something, but I ignored her.

"We were seated at the rear of the room," I told her. "It's my policy to sit in that location to observe the crowd and to evaluate the presentation based on the responses of the audience."

Priscilla tried to speak again. I kept rolling.

"Frankly, I'm not surprised you didn't see us," I told her. "I questioned the quality of their video equipment as soon as I walked into the room, and was disappointed by the technology in use. In fact, I have serious doubts about staging an event here at Severin. A number of attendees I've conferred with have made similar comments."

That last part wasn't true, but oh well.

Priscilla made some kind of noise, but I ignored her.

"As for your comment about us networking on behalf of L.A. Affairs, your concerns are premature," I went on. "I never consider blindly approaching other vendors, not until I've taken their measure, evaluated their ethics, and determined that they are the caliber of associates worthy of doing business with L.A. Affairs."

Priscilla didn't say anything.

"The management staff sent Kayla and me here because of our expertise," I said. "We are, in fact, networking with other vendors, finding the truth, not simply accepting what's explained in the workshops. Anyone can sit through a workshop, but I've determined that isn't good enough for L.A. Affairs, and I am proceeding in that vein."

It took everything I had not to keep going.

When I'm on a roll, I'm *really* on a roll.

"Well … all right," Priscilla said, in total back-down mode. "I can see you have things under control."

"Of course we do," I told her.

"Just … just keep me updated," she said.

"Frankly, Priscilla, all of this texting you're doing is intrusive and disruptive," I said. "I'll keep you updated, as time permits."

I ended the call and, somehow, kept myself from doing a fist pump and Snoopy happy dance combo.

Kayla and Rosalind both stared at me with their mouths open.

"I'm kind of afraid of you now," Rosalind mumbled. "But in a good way."

"Wow, awesome," Kayla said.

I handed Kayla's phone back to her. "Please tell me there's not another workshop starting now."

"Lunch in the main dining room. I'm heading for the bar," she said, and took off.

I wished I could go with her but Rosalind was still standing at my elbow and I couldn't let her get away without questioning her.

The crowd in the corridor thinned out, thanks to the big rush to the dining room for lunch. Rosalind glanced around, then leaned a little closer.

"I have to talk to you about Elita's ... about what happened to her," she said softly. "You think I'm involved, don't you? You think I had something to do with it."

I could have pounced on her, peppered her with questions and accusations—especially while I was still on a high from putting the smack-down on Priscilla—but I knew I had to handle Rosalind differently.

"Do you have an alibi?" I asked, in my I'm-on-your-side voice.

"I was in my room ... alone," she said. "I needed to get away."

"From Elita?" I asked.

I remembered how Elita had presented Rosalind like a trophy in a big game hunt to everybody they encountered, and had thrown a complete fit about changing her booth for Rosalind's cooking demo.

"Elita could be kind of ... you know, a little pushy," Rosalind admitted.

"More than a little?" I said.

"Well, yes. She knew I didn't want to work at her B&B after I won the cooking championship. But she said if I didn't, word would get out and it would be this big media firestorm, and then the network would never let me be on another show, or have a show of my own."

"It was crappy of her not to let you out of your contract," I said.

Rosalind managed a small, appreciative smile.

"Were you involved in Elita's death?" I asked. "Did you murder her?"

Rosalind twisted her fingers together. "I didn't wish her any harm, despite everything."

"The police might see it differently," I pointed out.

She gasped.

"You had motive. You knew when Elita was going through the labyrinth. You don't have an alibi," I said. "You look guilty."

Rosalind stared at me.

I stared back.

Rosalind kept staring.

"I can go over it again, if you'd like," I offered.

Rosalind shook her head frantically. "I just wish … oh, I just wish this whole thing would go away."

She darted down the corridor.

I watched as Rosalind disappeared around the corner and thought about her wish that this situation *would go away*. Not exactly the fiery declaration of someone capable of murder—even after everything Elita had done. But still, Rosalind hadn't denied involvement in Elita's death.

As much as I wanted to head for the bar and join Kayla in a glass of wine, I needed to keep a clear head and I needed to eat. Hopefully, today's luncheon would include something mega chocolatey for dessert.

I wound my way through the building to the dining room crowded with dozens of circular tables that seated eight, and a podium at the front of the room. Obviously, some sort of presentation was planned after lunch was served. I'd have to eat fast so I could make my escape if the talk turned out to be boring.

I found my designated table and joined the other men and women already seated. Introductions were made and we chatted as the food was served, a typical banquet meal of meat, veggies, hot rolls, and beverages that tasted as good as a meal can when prepared for hundreds of guests.

Dessert was a major disappointment.

"What? No chocolate?" I asked, eyeing the slice of apple pie the server set in front of everyone.

"What's this all about?" another woman at the table remarked, frowning.

The gal beside me said, "If it's not chocolate, it's not dessert."

"I would never stage an event that didn't include chocolate," I declared, poking at the flaky crush with my fork. "I always feature a huge dessert bar. Massive quantities of chocolate, of course."

"You're my kind of planner," another woman said.

None of the men at the table commented and were actually eating the pie.

Honestly, I don't get men sometimes.

I was already feeling the effects of not having my favorite drink in the world—a mocha frappuccino—from the most fabulous place in the world—Starbucks—so no way could I eat a dessert that primarily consisted of fruit. I mean, really, fruit.

Just as I was planning my excuse to leave the table, my phone rang. I made my apologies and fished it out of my handbag as I walked out of the dining room, and saw that Mom was calling. I paused—mentally and physically—debating on whether I should put off this conversation, then decided it was better to get it over with.

I mean that in the nicest way.

"Do you have the information?" Mom asked.

Note—she didn't ask how I was, where I was, or what I was doing. That's my mom.

"What have you learned?" she asked.

I had no idea what she was talking about, but felt sure it had something to do with selling our family home.

"I need you to get back to me with that information I asked you to check on," Mom said. "Things are happening fast."

My anxiety level amped up as I envisioned a staging crew descending on our house, a Realtor caravan rolling up, multiple offers pouring in.

"Things? What things?"

"Well, things," Mom insisted. "I have a hair appointment, plus I had to schedule a massage for this evening."

Okay, so really nothing was happening.

"So you'll get me that information?" Mom asked.

I still had no idea what I was supposed to do for her, so what could I say but, "I'm all over it, Mom."

"Wonderful," she said, and hung up.

So even though nothing was really happening and the sale of our family home didn't seem to be going anywhere, I knew my brother and sister would want to be kept in the loop. I dashed off messages to both of them. Even though we were all busy with our own lives, and time and distance kept us from being close, I found myself wishing they were here. I could really use some backup if this thing with Mom and the house ever gained any momentum.

I accessed the conference schedule and saw that the upcoming workshop was something I might actually want to attend—and pay attention to. It was titled *Preparing for the Unthinkable: Unexpected Complications and How to Overcome Them,* and was presented by a major event planning company in New York.

I tapped out a quick text message to Kayla letting her know I'd meet her there, then headed toward the main corridor and spotted Charles Kent standing along the wall just ahead of me, staring off at nothing.

When I'd seen him earlier in the exhibit hall talking with Mindy at the L.A. Affairs booth, he'd told me he knew Elita had been murdered—informed of the news by an acquaintance. I didn't need Scooby-Doo investigative skills to know he might provide a major clue.

I stopped next to Charles and offered what I felt was a warm, non-threatening greeting. He gave me a warm, non-threatening response.

"Are you enjoying the conference, Haley?" he asked, and made it sound as if he were performing Shakespeare.

"I am," I told him. "How about you?"

"I always enjoy the conference, year after year," he said.

Wow, Charles must have had a super successful business if he was invited back regularly.

"This is the first year L.A. Affairs has received an invitation," I said.

"Ah," he said, nodding. "You must be very excited about Friday."

Okay, that was a weird comment. Friday was the last day of the conference.

Anyway, I pushed on to the real reason I wanted to talk to him.

"When we spoke earlier, you mentioned you'd heard about Elita's death from an acquaintance," I said.

"And you learned of it, too?" he asked, frowning.

"I discovered her ... the crime scene," I explained.

"Oh, dear. How horrible for you, Haley," he said.

"Was it someone here at the conference who told you? Management seems to be going to great lengths to keep it quiet."

"Yes, quite right. They're keeping it quiet, as they should." Charles nodded slowly, like a wise old owl making a grave determination on something. "I understand your concern. If word got out of your unfortunate involvement, you'd garner unwanted attention—questions, callous remarks, that sort of thing. I'm sure that's not what you want to be remembered for here at the conference."

"So you learned of Elita's death from an acquaintance, not someone here?" I asked.

"Well, yes and no."

Charles settled into his story, as if he were seated in a brocade wingback chair, clutching a pipe, surrounded by shelves of leather bound first editions.

"I've known Parnel for many years. Old friend. Back when he was married to Claire, his first wife. Lost her to cancer. Nasty business," he said. "The girls, their three daughters, were devastated, of course. Tough time. Tough time for everyone."

"So that's who told you about Elita?"

"If only that were possible. No, unfortunately Parnel suffers from health problems. In a care facility for some time now. Hard to see an old friend struck down." Charles shook his head gravely. "I learned of Elita's demise from Shannon."

Either that was a weird coincidence, or something even weirder was going on.

"Shannon?" I asked. "Shannon Alda? Who works here?"

"Yes, Shannon, Parnel's daughter," Charles said. "Elita didn't take Parnel's last name when they married, something about maintaining her business persona, such as it was. I had no idea Shannon worked here until I happened to run into her yesterday. I could see she was troubled, so she told me what had happened to Elita."

Okay, well, that explained why none of the family had come to the conference center—Shannon was already here. It explained, too, why Shannon had been so upset and hadn't been able to deal with Kayla and me after finding Elita's body. I was amazed she could keep working at all, knowing her stepmom had been murdered pretty much right under her nose.

Wow, talk about a double whammy. Shannon had surely been instrumental in securing an invitation for Elita to attend HPA, especially when her B&B wasn't even operating yet. She gets her stepmom in the door, then she's murdered here. Yikes!

Charles glanced at his wristwatch. "I must be off. Another workshop awaits."

He smiled and nodded, and walked away.

I stood there, a wave of oh-my-God reverberating through me. Shannon must have an iron core to be able to continue with her responsibilities here at Severin at a time like this. Either that or she didn't want to face her two sisters, knowing how she'd indirectly been responsible for their stepmother's death.

"Haley—Hannah? Haley. Yes, Haley?"

Mindy appeared next to me, her cheeks flushed, craning her neck to see past me. I followed her line of sight and spotted Charles strolling away with the crowd.

"Am I imagining it, or have you got the hots for Charles?" I asked.

She blushed and giggled. "Oh, no. Of course not."

"Really?"

"Well, he is a very charming man," she said, the waved her hands as if to wipe her words from the air. "I've known him for years—well, I've known *of* him. Our social circles intersected from time to time, back when I was married."

"Is Charles married?"

"Oh, no. No, no, no. Not anymore."

From the deep frown on Mindy's face I sensed major gossip was forthcoming—which I was always up for, regardless of the circumstances.

"What happened?" I asked.

"His wife left him," Mindy said, shaking her head. "They got a divorce. It nearly killed Charles financially, from what I heard.

Then she took all that settlement money and invested it, and lost every cent. All because of Edith—Elita."

A few seconds passed while I tried to sort out what she'd just said. Mindy didn't seem to notice, nor did she hold back on the gossip.

"I heard that Elita had instigated their separation, then their divorce," she went on. "Of course, things must not have been good between them, if that happened. Still, there was a feeling among most of our crowd of friends that Elita pushed her into it, then convinced her to invest in her new business, the one that went bust."

"Elita contrived to end Charles's marriage?" I asked, just to be sure I understood. "Then she convinced his ex-wife to put all of her settlement money into Elita's business, and she ended up losing everything?"

"Yes," Mindy told me. "I heard that Charles was livid, absolutely livid. I'm glad to see he's over it now."

I gazed down the corridor and glimpsed Charles as he turned the corner.

I wasn't so sure he was over it.

Likely, he'd seen Elita parading Rosalind around on the first day of the conference. He was probably stunned to see her here. He might have seen her booth and known she was opening another business. It might have brought the whole divorce back to him. He'd been at the conference for years, knew this was Elita's first time here and that she would be among the first to go through the labyrinth.

He had motive—a heck of a motive. He had opportunity. Though he was graying, he looked fit enough to swing a shovel with deadly force.

I was pretty sure I'd found another murder suspect.

CHAPTER TEN

I woke the next morning thinking about Shannon and not feeling so great about myself—not the best way to start a new day.

I rolled out of bed and got ready ahead of Kayla—today I selected a navy blue pinstripe suit and jazzed it up with a Betsy Johnson shoulder bag—and told her I'd meet her at the first workshop, then left our room. The breakfast station was set up in the main corridor again this morning, so I grabbed a cup of coffee and a pastry—wishful thoughts of a mocha frappuccino from Starbucks dancing in my head—and found a spot at one of the tall tables. I definitely needed a caffeine and sugar boost to tackle my morning.

The thing with Shannon was really bothering me. I'd ratted her out to Olivia for totally ignoring Kayla and me after finding Elita's body, and gotten her into trouble—and all along it was Shannon's own stepmother who'd been murdered.

Of course, I hadn't known that at the time. Obviously, Shannon had been trying to carry on. Maybe staying on the job at the conference center was easier than facing her sisters and the rest of her family. Maybe she was too overcome with guilt for arranging Elita's presence at the place that got her murdered. It seemed odd to me that she would continue working even under those circumstances, but who was I to judge? People handled situations—especially anything to do with family—in different ways.

Getting Shannon into trouble with her supervisor was surely that one extra thing she hadn't needed to deal with. I owed her an apology.

The crowd milling around and moving through the main corridor seemed tense this morning. Day three of the conference meant the newness had worn off, and the workshops, luncheons, and events seemed like a grind. Some people would start to miss their loved ones, others would worry about what was happening at their jobs, and most everyone would be concerned about all the work that was piling up in their absence. Tomorrow, everyone would lighten up because the end would be in sight. We just had to get through today.

After I finished my coffee and pastry and dumped my trash, my cell phone rang. Ty's name appeared on the caller ID screen. I cringed slightly—not a good sign. He wanted to talk about our last conversation at my apartment, the one that had turned my world upside down. I'd put him off. No way was I up to dealing with it now—not with the Shannon thing uppermost in my mind. I let his call go to voicemail.

I headed down the main corridor and into the exhibit hall. I didn't know where I'd find Shannon this morning but I figured this was a good place to start. I didn't want to text her with a request to meet, figuring she'd think I wanted to complain to her about something else. Not a good way to start off an apology.

I spotted Zander right away—jeez, that guy must have already walked a hundred miles pushing that cart through the exhibit hall—loaded down with more brochures for the vendor booths. I fell in step beside him.

"Seriously, you ought to ask for some help with this job," I said.

He gave me a big smile and waved one hand around. "This is my domain and I am its king."

I couldn't help but smile. Zander seemed to really love what he was doing.

"I'm looking for Shannon," I said. "Have you seen her this morning?"

He thought for a few seconds, then shook his head. "Not this morning. Not yesterday. Monday. Yeah, late on Monday. Saw her talking to this year's problem vendor. There's always one."

"You mean Elita Winston? From the B&B?" I asked.

"That's the one," Zander said. "Shannon is pretty easy going—you know, as easy going as anybody can be at this place—but even she couldn't make that woman happy. If I see Shannon I'll let her know you're looking for her."

"Thanks," I said, as he headed down the aisle.

Before I could even take in what Zander had said, Shannon appeared in the crowd. She seemed surprised—and not the least bit pleased—to see me.

She walked over, her shoulders straight, her chin up. She still looked pale and stressed, same as when I'd seen her before. But now I knew it was for a different reason.

"Hello, Haley. Do you need anything? Is there something I can help you with?" she said, with enough chill in her voice to freeze me on the spot.

"Look," I said. "I'm sorry I complained about you and got you into trouble with Olivia. I didn't know Elita was your stepmother."

Shannon's already rigid frame seemed to lock up tighter.

"I wouldn't have said anything, if I'd known you two were related," I went on. "I can only imagine how guilty you must feel, pushing to get her the invitation to attend the conference and then she's—"

"I had nothing to do with that." Shannon blasted the words at me. "I didn't know she was coming to the conference. I had no idea she'd be here. I was totally surprised to see her name on the brochure."

I guess she was talking about the brochure she'd showed Kayla and me at the messenger bag giveaway display when we'd arrived at the conference. I remembered that she'd seemed kind of weird when Zander had delivered them. Now I knew why.

"You saw her here, right?" I asked, remembering the remark Zander had made. "You two talked about that new B&B of hers?"

"It isn't *hers*," Shannon insisted. "It belongs to—"

She clamped her mouth shut and gave herself a little shake. "As I said, let me know if I can assist you or Kayla in any way."

She pushed past me without another word.

I didn't know if Shannon plain old didn't like me—she'd totally blown off my apology—or if something else was going on.

As I left the exhibit hall and headed down the main corridor, I tried to put the pieces together in my head. Zander had seen Shannon and Elita talking Monday before the labyrinth walk, and said that they both seemed upset. Was it because of all of Elita's demands for changes—reprinting the messenger bag swag brochures, redoing her booth for the cooking demo? Did Shannon think it reflected badly on her, since Elita was her stepmother?

Nobody wanted to be associated with *that* person.

Maybe it was simply the shock of finding out her stepmother was participating in the conference that had upset Shannon. Apparently, Elita hadn't let her know she'd be here. What did that say about their relationship? Did that mean it was bad—bad enough to turn deadly?

The thought buzzed in my head as I turned down the hallway, moving along with the flow of other people heading for the workshop.

Should I consider Shannon a murder suspect? She knew when Elita would go through the labyrinth. She knew the layout of convention center grounds. She appeared physically able to wield a shovel with deadly force.

Obviously, I needed more info.

I grabbed my phone and called the hottest homicide cop in L.A.

***

I managed to get through the two morning workshops without dozing off. It helped that Kayla was there and we passed notes back and forth sharing our opinions of some of our L.A. Affairs co-workers—yeah, just like in sixth grade. Liam sent me a text asking how I was doing and saying that he missed me, which was really nice; I responded that I missed Starbucks—and him, of course—along with lots of emojis. Then my morning got a mega-boost when Jack texted asking if I'd have lunch with him.

When the workshop broke up, Kayla was totally onboard with me blowing off the official conference luncheon—she knew how hot Jack was—and promised to cover it for us. I hit the restroom, freshened my makeup and fluffed my hair—yes, I know, my lunch with Jack was all about business but so what—then found him waiting at a table in the small dining room at the rear of the conference center.

He looked awesome in yet another suit and tie. He rose when I approached and held my chair for me—I don't know how that got to be a custom but I liked it—and sat down again.

The restaurant was about half full, since most everyone was in the official HPA luncheon. The atmosphere was subdued, reflecting the cream and pale blue color scheme, and the pastoral murals. One wall was sets of French doors that provided a spectacular view of the landscaped grounds and gardens, and a glimpse of the tennis courts and the helipad.

"How's it going?" I asked.

"It could be better," he said.

The waiter stopped at our table.

"I don't suppose you serve Starbucks here, do you?" I asked.

The closest thing to a grin I'd seen in a long time pulled at Jack's lips. He knew about my frappie addiction. *Everybody* knew.

"No, sorry," the waiter said.

Jack ordered an iced tea—though he looked like he sure as heck could use a beer—and I did the same.

I dived right in, hoping to perk up his day.

"Did you know that Elita Winston's stepdaughter works here at the conference center?" I asked.

Jack nodded. "I've spoken with Shannon several times."

"She's asking about the investigation?"

"The cops won't tell her anything," he said.

"What did you think of her?" I asked, remembering how I'd added Shannon to my mental list of suspects.

"Stressed, upset, worried. Just what you'd expect."

"Shannon could have been stressed, upset, and worried because her stepmother had been killed—or feeling those same things because she'd murdered her," I said, then told him what I'd learned about Shannon and the reasons—slim as they were—for suspecting her.

"Motive?" he asked.

"Nothing firm," I had to admit.

Jack shrugged. He didn't seem to think much of my concern over Shannon as a suspect, and I couldn't blame him.

The server brought our drinks and we ordered lunch. Jack got a steak sandwich. I wanted one, too, but asked for a salad instead. Women were supposed to order a salad. I don't know how that custom got started but I wished it would go away.

"What's the latest in the investigation?" I asked.

"A possible lead," Jack said. "A report was filed a few months ago, but no arrest was made. Elita called the police after a verbal confrontation."

"With who?"

Jack pulled his phone from the pocket of his jacket and swiped through the screens.

"The owner of a hotel chain. Charles Kent," he said.

My senses jumped to high alert. Oh my God, I'd been suspicious of Charles. Maybe I was right and I'd found the killer.

If Jack had learned about a confrontation between Elita and Charles that had resulted in a police report, the homicide detectives on the case knew, too, and had probably questioned him. I wondered why he hadn't mentioned it when I spoke to him about Elita earlier?

"He's here. At the conference. I talked to him," I said.

I gave Jack the rundown on what I'd learned from Mindy, how Elita had been instrumental in ending Charles's marriage and leaving him in a financial bind, then causing his ex to lose all of her settlement money in Elita's failed business venture.

"I could imagine Charles running into Elita somewhere, and his temper finally boiling over into a verbal confrontation. It must have been pretty bad if the police were called," I said.

"Money pushes people to do things they wouldn't ordinarily think of doing," Jack said.

"Maybe those old feelings heated up between them again on Monday when he saw her here at the conference," I said.

"Maybe," Jack said, and I could see he was thinking it over.

The server came with our lunches. I eyed Jack's hearty sandwich with envy, then started on my salad.

"Since there's no indication of criminal ties or activity," Jack said, "the motive for Elita's murder must be something personal."

"Elita seems like she was kind of a bully," I said. "She forced Rosalind, her supposed friend, to blow off a huge opportunity and work at her B&B. She snubbed her old friend Mindy. She interfered with Charles' marriage to the point of ruining it. She convinced a friend to invest in her business then it sank. She didn't bother to let her stepdaughter know she'd be at the place she worked, then made her look bad to everyone here. And that's just the stuff I know about."

Hearing myself lay it out like that made Elita sound even worse. I don't want to say somebody deserved to die, but jeez.

Jack still seemed super stressed while we finished our lunches, and I felt like a semi-failure because I hadn't come up with anything definitive that would lead to Elita's murderer. I had several suspects and a lot of *maybes*, none of which were getting us anywhere.

"Looks as if the stolen messenger bags are long gone," Jack said, as he signed our lunch tab.

I was surprised he brought it up since it wasn't big on his radar, compared to Elita's murder investigation.

"The stockroom is massive. Employees and outside vendors coming and going. The only surveillance footage is at the exits, and there are multiple exits. Those bags could have been smuggled out of the building dozens of ways," Jack said, and looked pretty defeated.

"The bags weren't locked up?"

I figured the stockroom had a cage for high-end items, mainly the expensive liquors served in the bar and restaurants. At a couple thousand a pop, the Titan bags sure as heck qualified as expensive.

"They were in boxes, and stored in the minimum security area. A number of people have access to the keys." Jack looked annoyed at the measures that had been put in place—obviously, not his decision.

"So whoever stole the bags knew where they were stored, and how to get to them," I said.

"Severin security has handled these types of giveaways before, with no problems," Jack said, and his shoulders slumped. "There's no way to trace the bags."

I figured the swag vouchers inside the bags had been trashed, so there wasn't even a hope of finding the thief if someone came forward to claim one of the giveaways.

"The bags could be anywhere by now," Jack said.

He looked grim. His professional reputation and his business were circling the drain, taking his future along with it.

I reached across the table and laid my hand on his.

"We'll get this figured out," I told him.

He turned his wrist and captured my fingers in his. His skin was warm, his grip just strong enough to make my toes curl a little.

"Sure we will," he said.

He sounded strong, but I saw the look in his eyes. He wasn't sure we'd figure it out—not sure at all. Not sure he'd survive this, not sure things would ever be the same again.

No way would I let that happen. I was going to find Elita's murderer, no matter what it took.

CHAPTER ELEVEN

I spent the afternoon in workshops, but really wasn't listening to much of what was being said. My head was filled with murder.

While the speakers droned on, I pulled out my conference-issued notepad and wrote down the names of my suspects. I noted some common threads linking them to the crime. All of them knew the deal with the labyrinth walk. All of them were physically strong enough to swing a shovel with deadly force. All of them had motive—varying degrees of motive, but who's to say how much was enough to push someone over the edge?

Rosalind was the front runner, of course. I figured Charles Kent was an obvious second. Shannon's reasons for being on the outs with Elita seemed slim, but they had that whole family thing going, and everybody knew what it was like dealing with family. My suspicion of Olivia put her fourth on my suspect list, and a distant fourth at that. I considered marking her off, but decided what the heck and left her name there.

As far as I could see, all of my suspects had personal reasons to dislike, maybe even hate Elita, to the point of either initiating a confrontation or being caught up in an escalating situation that resulted in her death.

But why now? Why here? Why at the conference?

All of my suspects—except for I'm-not-so-sure-about-her Olivia who'd only just met Elita, as far as I knew—had known Elita for a long time, so it seemed her death was a crime of opportunity. Something had happened that spurred her murderer into action. Whoever it was had seen something, heard something, or learned something on Monday that had caused him or her to do the unthinkable. Somehow, there'd been a final straw and they couldn't tolerate Elita any longer.

But what was it?

By the time the last workshop ended, my brain was tired. All my who-did-it-and-why thoughts had worn me down. My day definitely needed a boost. Where was a Starbucks when I desperately needed one?

Kayla and I moved along with the crowd, everyone fanning out in the corridor, going for their phones or chatting about the class. I hadn't heard from anyone at L.A. Affairs lately—thank God that Priscilla had actually backed off—and I needed to find out what was up with Nadine and my events.

"I'll catch up with you later," I said to Kayla.

"I'll be in the bar," she said.

I dug out my phone as I stepped out of the flow of people and saw that I had a call from Ty. I'd missed it while I was in the workshop thinking about murder suspects—a topic only marginally more troubling than the thought of actually talking to my ex-official boyfriend.

I'm pretty sure that said something about my feelings for Ty's we-have-to-talk campaign, but since I hadn't had any sugar or caffeine lately, I wasn't positive.

Anyway, the best I could do was send him a text message. I explained that I was elbow-deep in conference duties on behalf of L.A. Affairs—if there was anything Ty understood it was that business came before anything else—and that I would get back to him as soon as I could. I tried to include a string of emojis to prove everything was okay, but couldn't bring myself to tap them out.

My energy level was low and dealing with Ty didn't help anything, but my jeez-I-know-I-have-to duties weren't done. I had to talk to Nadine about my events.

I called her. As soon as I spoke, she put me on hold.

I'm starting to really not like Nadine.

"Look, Haley," she said, when she came back on the line. "I've got your events under control—finally."

Finally? *Finally?*

"So stop hounding me." Nadine hung up.

Okay, now I officially hate Nadine.

Just as I was about to call her back, my phone buzzed and I saw my mom's name on the ID screen. Not exactly the great pick-me-up I needed. Still, better to get it over with. No way did I want a return call from Mom hanging over me.

"Great news," Mom announced.

I doubted it but didn't say so.

"We've had showing after showing," Mom said. "It's incredible, really."

"Showings? What do you mean showings?"

"The house," she said.

"People are there? *Already?*"

Strangers were in our house? Looking at our things, touching them? I felt violated, somehow.

"My agent is thrilled," Mom said.

"But I thought—"

"She says I can expect this to continue," Mom said.

"More showings?" I might have yelled that.

Mom didn't notice.

"So give me a call with that information I need first thing in the morning," she said, and ended the call.

Oh my God. *Oh my God.* This couldn't be happening. It couldn't. Of all things for Mom to actually stick with, to follow through on, it had to be selling our family home?

I realized I was walking aimlessly through the main corridor, still clutching my phone. I realized, too, that I had to do something about this situation. I wasn't sure where my dad was on this whole thing. More than likely, he'd blown off Mom's talk of selling and had expected her to give the idea her usual brief flirtation then move on, pretty much the same as I had done. My brother and sister were both overseas, too far away to intervene effectively when, apparently, more buyers were expected to pour in.

So it was all on me.

I headed for the front of the conference center, texting as I went, and got my car from the valet. As I pulled away, I glimpsed the air crew milling around the helipad, and wished I could get a ride with them—but only if they could stop by Starbucks on the way.

***

I bypassed a lot of Starbucks as I headed east on the 101 because I knew my favorite mocha frappuccino was waiting for me. I'd texted Detective Shuman—L.A.'s hottest homicide detective—and he'd agreed to meet me on my way to Mom's house. He even knew which Starbucks to go to—that's how well we knew each other.

I exited the freeway on Hayvenhurst, then turned onto Ventura Boulevard and pulled into the parking lot. It was almost dark but the street was busy and lit up like daylight, so I spotted Shuman right away seated at a table inside. He was a little older than me, with dark hair and a good build, a boy-next-door kind of look, and had on his usual shirt-tie-jacket combo. He grinned when he saw me get out of the car—Shuman's got a killer grin.

We'd known each other for a while and had helped out with a few investigations. There was some sort of heat between us, but what with our assorted girlfriends and boyfriends we'd never acted on it—not officially, anyway. Like me, Shuman was all about having one special person in his life. Another reason he was a cool guy.

Shuman rose when I approached and did the manly chair-holding thing while I sat down. A venti mocha frappuccino was already on the table for me; he had his usual black coffee.

"So you're involved in another murder?" Shuman asked, as he sat down across from me.

I could see he wanted to get right to it. He was doing me a huge favor by carving out a few minutes from either an investigation or his personal time to meet me. I wanted to roll with it but took a long drink of my frappie instead.

I sighed. "I've been craving one of these like crazy."

He raised his eyebrows. "No Starbucks at the convention?"

"No, and I sure as heck could have used one after I found that dead body," I said.

I hadn't mentioned in my initial text to Shuman that I was asking for his help because of Jack Bishop. He hadn't asked for my reasons then, and didn't seem interested now—or maybe he was just used to me being involved in murders.

"Have you learned anything you can share?" I asked.

"Not much to share," Shuman said with a shrug. "The detectives assigned to the case haven't uncovered much. No suspects. No motive."

I got a little thrill that the detectives, with all of their resources, hadn't come up with a motive, either—and my four maybe-could-be suspects were looking pretty darn good right now. Still, maybe the cops knew something they were keeping quiet about.

"No suspects at all?" I asked.

"They looked at the family first," Shuman said. "The victim had no children of her own, three stepdaughters from her marriage to Parnel Alda. Two of them are married with kids, devoting themselves to mom-things. Both have alibis."

"The other daughter, Shannon, works at the Severin Center," I said. "She claims she didn't know Elita was attending the conference until she saw her name on one of the brochures."

"Nothing's turned up on her," Shuman said. "The husband, Elita's third—"

My brain lit up—and it wasn't because of the frappuccino.

"Elita was married twice before?"

There's nothing wrong with taking a few stabs at trying to find wedded bliss, but come on. Three marriages? At some point, you have to wonder what the heck was really going on.

"Number three had a stroke shortly after they were married," Shuman said. "He's been in a care facility ever since. You can't ask for a better alibi than that."

I took another hit of my frappie. It seemed that Elita had been attempting to make the best of a bad situation by opening the B&B, and carry on with life without her husband. Surely she'd envisioned a brighter future for them both.

"What about Charles Kent?" I asked. I'd mentioned his connection to Elita in my earlier message to Shuman.

"The verbal altercation between Kent and the victim," Shuman said, nodding. "A report was filed. Nothing more came of it. But it was one hell of a confrontation, according to witnesses."

It was hard to imagine calm, sedate Charles Kent duking it out verbally with Elita. But that's the kind of thing a person would do when pushed too far.

"Was Rosalind Russo questioned?" I asked.

"Questioned, but not a suspect."

Okay, that seemed kind of weird. I'd put Rosalind at the top of my suspect list.

"Did the detectives pin down an alibi for her?" I asked.

"They were vague on that," he said.

I could imagine Rosalind falling completely apart in front of the homicide detectives. On the surface, she didn't seem a likely suspect. I mean, really, she'd been too timid to stand up to Elita and get out of her B&B contract, so I could see how the detectives might have a tough time imagining her hitting Elita over the head with a shovel.

"What about employees at Severin?" I asked, hoping he'd mention Olivia.

"Nothing."

I sighed. "Wow, when you said the detectives didn't have much, you weren't kidding."

Shuman gave me a good natured I-told-you-so grin. I couldn't think of any other questions—even with the infusion of chocolate and caffeine from my frappuccino.

"Well, thanks for the help," I said.

I thought he might head out, but he sat there as if he wasn't in a hurry after all, so I figured this was a good opportunity to catch up—and maybe get some gossip.

"Are you still seeing Brittany?" I asked.

I noted that Shuman's attire looked a little more pulled together than usual, which made me think maybe he and Brittany had moved in together and she was dressing him. I liked Brittany, and I wanted Shuman to be happy. But I'd pictured her as his transition girlfriend—she's a lot younger than him—not someone permanent.

"Yes," he said, with a small smile that looked kind of sad.

"It's not going so well?"

"It's not really going anywhere," he admitted. "What about you? Still seeing that lawyer?"

"Liam. Yes, and it's kind-of going somewhere."

Shuman gave me a tell-the-truth frown I'm sure he'd perfected at the police academy.

"So you're done with your ex?" he asked.

"Ty," I said, and cringed slightly.

Shuman amped up his cop-stare and I caved.

"He came to my apartment," I said.

"He's back? Finally? After what, months? Some sort of sabbatical?"

I nodded. "He told me he was in love with me."

Yeah, just like that. Ty had shown up at my apartment—after no word from him *forever*—and hit me with the news. He loved me. After everything we'd been through, all the problems, the difficulties, the hurt, the breakup, he'd gone away to find himself and that's what he'd come up with.

Shuman looked as stunned as I had been that day when I'd looked up at Ty, who'd showed up out of the blue, standing in my living room, saying the words I'd wanted to hear for so long—only I'd been too shocked to react.

"Yep, that's what he told me," I murmured. "He loves me."

It was good to say the words aloud. I'd carried that whole thing around with me for a while now. I'd told Marcie on my way into work on Monday morning, but we hadn't had a chance to talk about it. And, really, I'd been trying hard not to think about any of it this week.

Shuman glanced away, as if the words had hit him hard—he knew Ty and I had had our ups and downs—then looked at me again.

"So, what did you say?" he asked.

"Ty didn't push me for a response. He said he wants me to think about our future together so we can discuss it."

"You're willing to do that?"

Here's where having this conversation with a BFF like Marcie would have been really different. She'd have been livid, or excited, or stunned, or something. We'd have analyzed every second of my conversation with Ty—what he said, how he said it, what his expression was when he said it—but not so with Shuman. With him, it was just a down and dirty Q&A. I was okay with it.

"He put his feelings for me out there, which is totally unlike him," I said. "I can't ignore that."

"You know what the past was like with him."

"He seems different now. Maybe the future will be different."

Shuman studied me for a long moment. "Do what's best for *you*."

His words and expression caused a funny little feeling in my belly.

"I will."

He gave me a lopsided grin. "You'd better."

I grinned back, then drained my frappuccino, and rose from the table.

Shuman got to his feet. "Let me know if you turn up anything else on the murder."

"I will," I promised.

I thanked Shuman for his help, and left.

But I still couldn't bring myself to think about Ty.

***

It was dark by the time I exited the 134 and wound through the hills to the small mansion that had been my home for as long as I could remember. Two security lights burned in the circular driveway. Several of the second-floor windows glowed yellow.

I'd driven here with the intention of confronting Mom, demanding to know what the heck she was thinking and how she could bear to sell our family home. I knew my brother and sister would have done the same, if they'd been here. I knew it was up to me to speak for all of us.

But somehow, I couldn't make myself get out of the car.

I gazed up at the house, at the window drapes I'd helped my mom pick out. Past them were the paint colors Mom had driven us all crazy selecting. She'd finally decided on pale blue for the den, and we'd all loved it. Our Christmas tree had stood in the same corner of the living room every year. In the dining room, we'd had holiday meals. The pool out back had been a constant source of family fun—swimming while my dad grilled burgers and Mom watched from a lounge chair in the shade.

A heaviness settled over me. I hadn't been very close with my younger sister, and my older brother was always too busy for me. Dad was often kind of distracted because of his work, and Mom—well, Mom was Mom. But thinking back now I recalled how many good times we'd had. Here, in this house. Together.

I could hardly stomach the thought of strangers buying our home, moving in, likely changing the paint color, ripping up the flooring, doing who-knows-what to the floor plan, the landscaping. Then I imagined those strangers changing nothing, using our things as if they were now theirs, and my stomach hurt worse.

My thoughts sped ahead into the future. Mom and Dad wouldn't be alive forever. Sooner or later the house would be sold. Eventually, my brother and sister and I would have to say goodbye to our family home. Things would change. They would end.

I stared up at the house, thinking of Mom and Dad inside, alone. Maybe it was sad for them. My sister stayed here occasionally, but really, all of their kids were gone. Maybe a new place would be good for them.

Maybe it was time to let go.

I drew in a long breath, thinking that, really, all of those wonderful family memories weren't in the house—they were in my head.

I started my car and drove away.

CHAPTER TWELVE

It was back to basics on Thursday morning. I dressed in another of my black business suits—really, you can't have too many black business suits—this one with a tiny white stripe, and paired it with a totally awesome Prada bag. Kayla had gotten up ahead of me and was already gone so I was on my own for coffee and pastries at the breakfast station in the main corridor. I spotted several women who worked at a caterer that I'd talked with during one of yesterday's workshops. They invited me to join them.

Always nice to be invited to join.

We chatted for a bit, then they headed for the morning's first session, anxious to get there early for seats up front. Weird, huh? Still, they were all really nice so I couldn't hold it against them.

I headed for the exhibit hall thinking I'd talk to Rosalind, question her, and get her to confess to murdering Elita. Yeah, I know, it was a long shot, but it was all I had at the moment. Tomorrow was Friday, the last day of the conference, the last day I'd have access to my suspects, the crime scene, the clues. If I didn't solve Elita's murder by then, my chances would be pretty darn low, and Jack's business reputation would continue its death spiral and maybe crash completely.

My heart did a little pitter-patter as I passed the Titan messenger bag on display. I still hadn't heard what was going to happen with the planned giveaway tomorrow. Maybe management was holding out hope the bags would be recovered in time for the closing session.

I spotted Rosalind at Elita's B&B booth, deep in conversation with Mindy. It was a little early for me to deal with Mindy, so I trekked through the aisles hoping I'd see Shannon or Olivia or Charles Kent; maybe I could get one of them to confess.

Instead I saw Zander coming out of the hallway that led to the stockroom, pushing his ever-present cart loaded with supplies for the vendors. No doubt about it, he was giving top-notch, Severin-quality service. He must have made a zillion trips to the stockroom this week. He was the only person responsible for replenishing the vendor booths, and not only had he done it with a smile, he'd even refused help. What a great employee.

Or was he?

An idea popped into my head, and grew larger. Zander was constantly in and out of the stockroom. His presence was routine—expected, really. He probably knew everyone who worked back there.

My footsteps slowed as Zander wheeled the cart down the aisle and disappeared.

Did he know someone well enough to help him steal and smuggle the Titan messenger bags out of the building?

My heart's pitter-patter picked up—but for a whole different reason.

I glanced around, saw no one watching, then headed down the hallway.

The passageway took a long, slow curve, designed to keep out prying eyes yet was wide enough to move supplies and equipment with ease. The thick carpet and soothing murals ended abruptly, giving way to a concrete floor and bare walls. The light grew brighter and the noise level amped up.

I stepped into the stockroom and gasped. Wow, this place was enormous—bigger than an aircraft hangar—and it was packed with supplies. I walked forward trying to take it all in.

Boxes—mountains of boxes, thousands of them—were stacked everywhere. Some of the shelving units reached the ceiling. There were supplies for the hotel guest rooms, the banquet room, the dining rooms, the break-out rooms—table linens, dishes, glasses, serving pieces, carts, tables and chairs. Another area held supplies for housekeeping—sheets, towels, tissues, tiny soaps and shampoo bottles. A huge corner was filled with vacuums, rug shampooers, and cleaning supplies. I spotted two cages, both padlocked. One held zillions of bottles of liquor and mixers, the other was packed with candy. I saw three huge doors that I figured were freezers and refrigerators.

There were three personnel doors and two loading docks. A laundry truck was backed up to one of the roll-up doors, and two guys were moving a mountain of dirty sheets from a gigantic bin into the truck. At the other door, another truck was being unloaded.

I spotted another cage, this one about half full of boxes, and figured it was the minimum security area the Titan bags had been stored in because the padlock dangled from a chain and the door stood open.

At least a dozen men and women moved through the aisles, gathering things, moving things, dumping things. Not one of them—not a single one—looked at me twice, asked why I was there, or what I was doing.

I headed back toward the hallway that led to the exhibit hall with the sure knowledge that the messenger bags could have been stolen and taken out of the stockroom with ease, any number of ways. Maybe Zander headed up, or was part of, a theft ring. Maybe a Casale lover had been overcome with the desire to roll around in bed with the four bags. There was no way to know. With the massive amount of supplies in the stockroom I doubted there was an inventory control system in place tight enough to track everything from Dom Perignon to miniature shampoo bottles. How would anybody know if something was taken, much less determine who had taken it?

Jack was right. Those bags were long gone, and there was little hope of discovering who took them, and no hope at all of recovering them.

Crap.

I passed through the exhibit hall—Rosalind and Mindy were no longer at the B&B booth—and headed down the main corridor feeling cranky and out of sorts. The Severin Center had lousy security measures in place for the Titan bags that had allowed them to be stolen—and now Jack's reputation would pay the price for it. And worse, there was nothing I could do to make it better, to help, and to restore Jack's good name.

My morning was off to a crappy start—not a good way to start the day. I needed to turn things around.

At that moment, I found myself longing to be in my office at L.A. Affairs. There was something about the routine, the familiarity, the I'm-in-charge that sounded good.

I decided to give Nadine a call and check up on the events I'd so perfectly planned for my clients. Maybe that would give my day a boost.

Of course, dealing with Nadine wasn't high on my oh-yeah-this-will-be-fun list, and our previous conversations had been difficult—Nadine seemed to know as much about event planning as the family pet. But I decided to give her another chance. After all, she was trying hard, putting in a lot of effort, and working toward getting promoted. I decided I'd approach her with a better attitude and surely she'd be in a better mood than the last two times I'd spoken with her.

I was wrong.

"Look, Haley," she snapped as soon as she answered my call, "these constant interruptions of yours are throwing off my entire day."

Okay, so much for my attempt at being positive.

"Here's what I'm dealing with," Nadine went on. "I'm upgrading the fortieth birthday party for Karen Vaughn. I want a carpet woven with her initials inside a heart, big enough to cover the entire venue. A confetti cannon that will explode when she blows out her candles. Then everyone will move outside where a hovering helicopter will shower guests with rose petals."

I glanced down at my phone, then put it to my ear again. Did I hear her correctly? Had she actually said those things—and thought they were good ideas?

"What the heck are you doing?" I said, and managed not to scream—at least, I thought I hadn't screamed. "Karen is a librarian. She's quiet, reserved. She doesn't want—"

"Oh, and Priscilla's been trying to hunt you down. And, believe me, she's not happy."

Nadine hung up.

Crap.

Bad enough I'd had to deal with Nadine, now Priscilla was looking for me. Jeez, could my day get any worse?

And then it did.

My phone rang. Priscilla was calling.

My already sour mood spiraled down to I-might-have-to-take-somebody-out. No way was I up to listening to Priscilla complain. But neither was I big on suspense.

"Yes, well, hello, Haley," Priscilla said when I answered. "I do certainly hope your day is going well and you're enjoying your time at the conference."

She was in total back-down mode. How weird was that?

"I just want to say once again how proud all of us here at L.A. Affairs are of you and Kayla," Priscilla went on. "Edie stopped me in the hall just yesterday and commented on it."

What the heck was going on with her?

"You're doing a fine job representing us at the conference," she said. "A very fine job."

Had she finally had a stroke sitting at her desk?

Thank God I wasn't in the office when it happened. No way did I want to be blamed for it—my personnel file couldn't take the hit.

"Yes, we're proud and pleased with everything you're doing," Priscilla said. "And I just know everything is going to go exceedingly well tomorrow."

"Tomorrow?" I asked.

"Yes. Tomorrow. Your presentation."

My ... what?

Priscilla said, "The last day of the conference is always the most exciting. It's when each first-time attendee takes the stage and delivers an in-depth report on their company."

An in-depth ...what?

"Edie and I discussed it and, of course, you were our first choice to give the presentation," Priscilla said, "because of your public speaking experience listed on your résumé."

My résumé? That stupid thing I'd filled out months ago? I'd put public speaking experience on it? And Edie—the head of HR—and Priscilla had believed it? What the heck was wrong with them? Everybody knew a résumé was total crap. It was expected, really. How would anybody ever get a job if they didn't lie about their qualifications?

"So, everyone here at the office has total confidence that your presentation in front of the hundreds of elite industry professionals—"

Everything Priscilla was saying turned into blah, blah, blah.

I launched into high-panic mode.

I had to get up in front of hundreds—*hundreds*—of people? *Elite* industry professionals? And give a speech? *Tomorrow?*

Yeah, okay, I was all right with public speaking. I could do it. But what the heck was I supposed to talk about? How was I going to get a talk prepared this quickly?

Something Priscilla said broke into my runaway thoughts.

"—video of our most prestigious events will play as you read the script," she said. "So just read the script. That's important. Follow the script. You'll do that, won't you, Haley? You'll follow the script we've prepared?"

She was starting to sound kind of nervous now. Like maybe she thought I'd try to wing it tomorrow in front of hundreds of people—which I might have to do since I had no idea where the script and the presentation video were.

Oh my God. *Oh my God.* I was bordering on total panic mode—but no way could I let Priscilla know.

Immediately, I channeled my mom's I'm-better-than-you voice, and said, "Yes, about that script."

"I know you've been rehearsing all week," Priscilla said.

Okay, so that must mean she'd sent everything to me when Kayla and I left L.A. Affairs on Monday.

Jeez, I really hope that's what it means.

"Everyone here is confident you'll do an outstanding job," Priscilla said. "Really. We're not worried. At all. Really. We're sure you'll do a fantastic job ... following the script."

Priscilla ended the call, but I hardly noticed. I'd hoped my day would get better yet it kept getting worse. And now I had to attend another workshop. But at least in there I could tune out most everything.

I found the workshop that was already underway and slipped into a chair on the back row. Instead of listening to the speakers, I frantically swiped through my messages from Priscilla and—thank

God—found everything she'd sent for the presentation I'd have to give tomorrow.

During the next workshop and lunch, I grabbed a few minutes to read over the script. Not exactly sizzling remarks likely to drive the elite industry professionals in the audience to the door of L.A. Affairs as if it were news of a 75% markdown at Nordstrom, so I wasn't sure why Priscilla had insisted I not wing it. Still, it would be easier for me if I just read the script. I could stand *easy* right now.

When the last workshop thankfully ended, Kayla and I headed down the corridor together.

"I say we hit the bar," she said.

I was just about to challenge her to a race to a table when my phone buzzed.

"I'll catch up with you," I said, and stepped to the side, out of the flow of everybody else who was likely headed for the bar.

I dug out my phone and saw that Mom was calling.

Great. Just what I needed at the end of a crappy day.

Still, there was a chance Mom had forgotten the whole idea of selling the house, giving my day the boost it desperately needed, so I answered.

"My agent is on the way over," Mom announced. "She's so excited. We have multiple offers on the house."

"What?"

Mom yammered on as if I hadn't screamed the word into the phone, but it all turned into blah, blah, blah.

There were offers on our home? For real? Someone—lots of people—wanted to buy it? Now? And we'd have to move out? Leave? Never come back? Just like that?

Memories exploded in my head. Blowing out birthday candles; my dad helping me learn to ride my new pink bike in the driveway; hanging out in my room with my friends; my prom date picking me up; my grandparents and cousins visiting. And now another family would be in *our* home, doing those same things?

Last night when I'd been at the house, I'd convinced myself that it was time to let go, to move on, and that I would be okay with Mom's decision to sell. But now that it was a reality—jeez, I didn't know if I could stand it.

I realized then that Mom had ended the call and I was staring at nothing, still holding my phone to my ear.

Oh, crap. Where were my brother and sister when I needed them? If they were here, we could triple-team Mom, maybe turn this thing around.

I shoved my phone into my handbag. Somehow, I was going to stop this sale. I'd have to do it alone. My brother and sister weren't here, but they were counting on me. I'd have to figure out something.

Fortifying myself with a glass of wine seemed a good way to get my brain cells hopping, so I headed to the bar. The place was crowded. All of the conference attendees seemed a little more relaxed and interested in partying since this was our last night here.

I spotted Kayla seated at a large table. With her were several men and women we'd met in the workshops and at other conference events, everybody laughing, talking, and knocking back drinks—my kind of crowd, usually. Also seated there was Mindy. Charles Kent was beside her. They sat close, their heads leaning together, shoulders touching, talking.

Great. Just what I needed to see.

While I was usually annoyed with life on Planet Mindy, I knew things had been tough for her since her husband left and she had to get a job and start over. Honestly, I wished things would improve for her, that she'd find a great place in life and would be happy.

Only now that it looked like she might have finally connected with someone, it was Charles Kent—the man I suspected of murder.

What the heck was I supposed to do? Go over there and break them up? Tell Mindy my suspicion? Keep her from making a huge mistake?

But what if I was wrong? Maybe Charles hadn't murdered Elita. Maybe he really was a great guy who'd make Mindy happy. If I said something, I would ruin everything.

Oh, crap.

I left the bar and went outside.

It was dark. The night air was cool. No one else was out. Twinkle and accent lights lit the walkway as I headed away from the conference center. I needed some peace, some tranquility, a respite from all the crappy things that had happened today, and found myself approaching the entrance of the labyrinth. No one was here, either, since it was closed for the night.

Then just ahead of me, barely visible in the pale moonlight, I spotted a figure dressed in black silently unclip the rope that stretched across the entrance, then disappear into the labyrinth.

My heart rate amped up. Oh my God. Was someone involved with Elita's death returning to the scene of the crime? The murderer? Who else would be sneaking around out here in the dark, entering the labyrinth after it was closed?

I sure as heck could use a break solving this crime. Maybe this was it.

At the entrance to the labyrinth I slipped off my pumps and headed down the walkway. My footsteps were silent as I hurried along, cautiously peering around every curve, trying to spot whoever was ahead of me.

I'd only been in the labyrinth once, but I knew I was getting close to the exit. I didn't want whoever was ahead of me to leave and disappear into the woods or make it back to the conference center before I identified them. I rounded the final curve and spotted no one. Darn. I rushed toward the exit and a giant jumped up in front of me.

I screamed and fell back. He grabbed my wrist. I swung my shoes at him but he blocked my arm. I was about to—well, do something. I didn't know what—but something—when I heard a familiar voice.

"Haley?"

I squinted up at him. "Jack?"

Oh my God. Jack Bishop. He had on a dark suit, shirt, and tie, making him almost invisible in the night.

He let go of my wrist, looking annoyed that I was in this isolated area, alone, in the dark.

"What are you doing here?" he demanded.

"What are *you* doing here?" I asked. "And why did you jump out at me?"

"I thought you were the murderer."

"I thought *you* were the murderer," I said.

"I didn't murder anybody."

"Neither did I," I said. "But I might murder you now for scaring the crap out of me."

I drew in a few big breaths, trying to calm myself, waiting for my heart rate to return to normal. Then I realized I was in an isolated area, in the dark, not alone, but with Jack.

No way would my heart rate slow down now.

"So, really, what are you doing out here?" Jack said, sounding reasonable now.

I clamped onto his arm and pulled on one shoe, then the other. Wow, he was solid. Strong. He smelled great.

"I just had to get away," I said.

"Me, too," he said, and heaved a heavy sigh.

I noticed then that Jack's collar was open and his tie was pulled down. He sounded tired, weary. Kind of like I felt.

"Not just get away, get far away," he said. "Maybe just say to hell with everything. Leave. Go somewhere else for a while."

That didn't sound like Jack. Obviously, everything he'd been through this week was weighing more heavily on him than I'd realized.

Then it hit me how much I wished I could just say to hell with everything, too. I wouldn't have to answer Ty's questions, give the presentation tomorrow, figure out my relationship with Liam, see our family home packed up and emptied—or do all the other things that seemed to be hanging over me all of a sudden.

"Alaska, maybe," Jack mused.

"I've always wanted to walk on a glacier," I said.

"You'd go?"

Something in his voice seemed to shoot right through me and set every nerve ending on fire. The night got quieter. The moon brighter. The breeze softer. And Jack—he suddenly looked stronger, sturdier, and even more handsome.

In that instant, I knew I wanted to walk on a glacier with Jack, like I'd never wanted to do anything else in my entire life.

He eased closer. "Would you?"

His cell phone rang. He ignored it.

"Would you go?" he whispered. "With me?"

"Tonight?" I asked, and my word came out in a breathy sigh.

His cell phone rang again. He whipped it out of his pocket and hit a button, silencing it.

"Tonight. Now," he said, easing even closer. "Right now."

"Leave? Walk away from everything?" I asked. "Could you do that, Jack? Really?"

"Hell yeah."

Just like that. No hesitation. No thinking it over.

Our gazes met and held.

His cell phone rang again. Jack growled under his breath, whipped it out of his pocket, pressed it to his ear and said, "What?"

He listened, frowned, then his brows drew closer together.

"I'll be right there." He put his phone away and looked at me, stunned. "The stolen messenger bags have been found."

The bags were so totally out of my thoughts, it took me a few seconds to understand what he said.

"Found? Where?"

"In the stockroom," he said. But instead of looking relieved, Jack looked more troubled.

"What?" I asked, then came back to the moment with a horrifying jolt of reality. "Are the bags okay? Did somebody damage them?"

"No." Jack shook his head, still looking bewildered. "The bags are fine. The swag inside of them is gone."

CHAPTER THIRTEEN

It was a Louis Vuitton day. Definitely a Louis Vuitton day.

It was also the last day of the conference.

The main corridor was nearly empty as I headed for the banquet room where the closing events would take place. I'd taken a little longer to get ready this morning, wanting to look my best standing in front of hundreds of elite industry professionals for the presentation I'd been pressed into giving. I'd gone with an I-take-my-work-seriously-but-I'm-still-fun up-do, a power red business suit, and completed my look with an I-have-excellent-taste Louis Vuitton bag.

Really, you can never go wrong with a Louis Vuitton bag.

Nor can your day go wrong after receiving a really nice text from your boyfriend. Liam had messaged me first thing this morning saying he missed me and had something special in mind for us. He'd often surprised me on our dates—so far, all of his ideas of a good surprise were the same as mine—so I was looking forward to learning what he had set up for us.

Jack popped into my head. Last night we'd talked about escaping, chucking everything, leaving all of our troubles behind. Of course, in the light of a new day everything looked different.

Damn. I hate it when that happens.

Honestly, remembering last night with Jack didn't make me feel so great about myself. I was all about having one special guy in my life and right now that was Liam—although I did still need to figure out what the heck to do about Ty and his we-need-to-talk revelation.

The image of the Titan messenger bags flew into my head as I turned down the hallway. I'd gone with Jack to the stockroom last night and, sure enough, there they were. All four of them, still in their boxes, in perfect condition—minus the swag that had been inside.

According to the Severin security guy who'd contacted Jack, they'd received an anonymous tip and located the bags hidden among a stack of similar-looking boxes—I guess the old saying is true: the best place to hide a book is in the library. Everybody, it seemed, was happy.

Except me. I kept wondering why all the swag wasn't inside the messenger bags. Why would someone leave the bags, but take the swag? It had no real value—it was just paper vouchers unlikely to be redeemed since the vendors knew they had been stolen—while the bags were crazy expensive.

Jack had given it an oh-well, not his problem, and the Severin security guys felt pretty much the same. Still, it bugged me.

I passed the banquet room's three sets of double doors, all closed, and spotted the sign beside them pointing to the green room. I slipped inside and saw comfy sofas, a couple of tables and chairs, and a buffet laid out with water, coffee, sodas, muffins, pastries, and other snacks including lots of chocolate, thank God.

Two other women were there whom I'd met in workshops, sitting separately, studying their phones, likely reviewing the presentations they'd give shortly. Kayla was there, too, along with Mindy. I was glad to see them both. A few butterflies fluttered in my stomach. Having friends there helped.

"Oh my God," Kayla said, rolling her eyes. "You're not going to believe who's here."

Okay, so that wasn't so helpful.

"I'm sure you're going to do fine," Mindy insisted. "No matter what."

Yikes! What the heck was going on?

Kayla nodded toward an open doorway and the short hallway that led to the banquet room. I peeked inside. The chairs were set up theatre style and were filled with hundreds of well-dressed, attentive, HPA attendees. A large stage fronted the room where a man stood at the podium giving a speech while scenes of a construction crew building an elaborate zombie-themed party played on a large screen behind him.

I spotted Priscilla seated on the front row.

Oh, crap.

"Why is she here?" I asked, as I hurried back across the room to Kayla and Mindy. "Did you know she was coming?"

"No way," Kayla said.

"Are you nervous?" Mindy asked.

I hadn't been—not until I saw Priscilla front and center, no doubt intending to follow my presentation word-for-word with the script she'd sent. And if she heard a deviation, did she intend to note it in my personnel file, mark it against me at my next employee review, or maybe jump up, rush the stage, and take over?

"I'm fine," I insisted—which was a total lie, of course.

"Don't worry, this will fix everything," Kayla insisted, and pulled a bottle of wine out of her tote bag. "Did you see who's sitting next to Priscilla?"

I'd been so shocked seeing her I didn't even notice anyone else.

"Edie," Kayla told me before I had a chance to look.

Yikes! Edie was here? Edie, the head of Human Resources at L.A. Affairs? Oh my God, did she intend to tag-team me with Priscilla if I went off-script? Yank me off of the stage when Priscilla took over my presentation, then fire me in front of the entire audience?

Shannon walked into the green room and headed straight for me. As my personal hostess, she was obligated to be here to make sure my presentation went off without a hitch.

Yeah, right.

I was already rattled, and her being here reminded me that I'd contributed to the upset in her life by complaining about her to Olivia.

As if to demonstrate how I'd added to her problems, Shannon looked really bad this morning—tense, grim, and a sickly pale that her half-hearted attempt at makeup application couldn't disguise. Now I felt really icky.

She stopped in front of me. I could see that being here and having to help me was a stretch for her. I couldn't blame her.

Now I felt even worse that I'd suspected her of murdering her own stepmother.

"Everything is ready for your presentation," Shannon told me, her words slow and measured. "Your speech will appear on the prompters, and your DVD will play on the screen behind you. Our tech guy is a professional. You can count on him."

"Thanks," I said. "Listen, Shannon, I really appreciate your coming here and making sure everything is set up and ready to go. I know you're under a lot of pressure, with what happened to Elita, plus your job—"

"No need to thank me," she insisted, and straightened her shoulders. "I'm taking a leave of absence effective immediately after your presentation, my last responsibility here."

Okay, that surprised me, and it made me feel even more crappy because she had to stay here until my speech was over. I figured her leaving had something to do with Elita's death—the funeral or a memorial service, or maybe she was just anxious to be with her sisters and the rest of her family.

Before I could thank her for hanging in here a while longer on my behalf, she whipped out her phone and walked to the other side of the room.

"You're up next," Mindy said, and gave me a concerned, mom-like pat on the shoulder. "Are you okay?"

"I'm okay," I said, without much enthusiasm. "I was just thinking about Shannon. She's leaving soon for a family thing."

"And that made you miss your family?" Mindy asked.

"Kind of," I admitted, then realized it was true. Mom had been blazing in my thoughts all week long, plus my brother and sister, while I wrestled with the prospect of our family home being sold.

"My mom put the house on the market—the place where I grew up—and it looks like it's going to sell fast," I said. "I know I shouldn't care. I don't even live there anymore, but—"

"Of course you should care," Mindy insisted. "The house is full of memories—good times, family holidays, things that can never come back. They're locked inside the house. Nobody wants another family living in their memories. It's a violation."

Okay, that kind of made sense—surprisingly so, coming from Mindy.

"But things have to change eventually, don't they?" I asked.

"Yes, things must go forward," Mindy agreed. "It was hard when my husband left and I had to move out of our home. It helped that I talked to other people who'd been through the same thing. Do you have brothers or sisters you could talk to about it? A friend, maybe? Someone who's family situation is changing?"

Before I could answer, Mindy's face lit up.

"Oh, I know," she announced. "You can talk to Shannon."

"What? No—"

"Shannon? Shannon?" Mindy rose on her toes and waved. "Could you come over here, please? Hannah needs you."

Oh, crap.

Shannon stomped over, gritting her teeth and shooting I-hate-you laser beams from her eyes straight at my heart.

If looks could have killed, I would have been a smoking hole in the floor.

"What is it?" Shannon ground out the words.

"Haley is upset about her parents selling their family home, and I know your dad and Elita decided to turn your family vacation home into a B&B," Mindy said. "Could you say something to Haley to make her feel better about—"

"It wasn't *Dad's* idea." Shannon fired the words as if they were engraved on a ballistic missile blasting skyward. "It was *her* idea. After he had a stroke. After he was in the care facility, when he couldn't do anything about it."

"Oh ...." Mindy drew back.

I leaned forward.

"The house in Lake Arrowhead." I said. "It was your family vacation home?"

"She might have married Dad, but the house belonged to the family—not her." Color rose in Shannon's cheeks. Her words poured out, bitter and angry. "My sisters and I, we talked to her, tried to reason with her, but no. She claimed it was *her* house now."

"Elita wanted to go ahead with the B&B, knowing the family objected?" I asked. "That was crappy."

"She promised she'd think it over, reconsider the idea—"

Shannon stopped suddenly, her gaze drilling Rosalind as she walked into the green room.

"What is *she* doing here?" Shannon demanded.

"She's doing a cooking demonstration," Mindy said.

"What?" Shannon's eyes blazed with renewed outrage.

"Haley?" A woman dressed in a Severin-cream business suit, clutching a tablet, approached. "You're on."

I heard applause in the banquet room.

"Break a leg," Mindy said.

"Give 'em hell," Kayla called, waving the wine bottle and looping my Louis Vuitton bag over her shoulder.

I waited in the hallway until the applause for the previous speaker died. A man who was acting as the emcee took the podium, gave a brief summary of L.A. Affairs, then introduced me. Applause rose as I climbed the stairs to the stage and settled in behind the podium.

As I gazed out over the audience I spotted all the people seated there whom I'd met this week, industry professionals I'd chatted with, exchanged phone numbers and email addresses with. A door at the rear of the room opened and Jack walked in. He looked more handsome than usual in a fantastic Tom Ford suit; his presentation was coming up later in the afternoon.

Always nice to see friendly faces in the crowd—plus a totally hot guy.

I flashed on last night when Jack and I were in the moonlit, secluded labyrinth, fantasizing about running off to Alaska. I wondered if he'd thought of it again—which was totally bad of me, I know.

Then my gaze snagged on Priscilla and Edie. They were seated on the front row, both dressed in we-can-squash-your-career business suits, their hair and makeup done to perfection. Still, Priscilla looked like she might have a stroke or, at minimum, a heart attack. I hoped Edie had brushed up on CPR and had one of those defibrillators tucked inside the Prada tote on the floor at her feet.

I greeted the audience, thanked HPA for inviting L.A. Affairs to the conference, and complimented the Severin team on all of their hard work putting on a fabulous event—and it was fabulous, except for the murder and the stolen messenger bags, of course.

I saw no need to mention that.

The tech guy seated at a table full of electronic equipment off to the side caught my eye. I nodded. He started the video presentation and I read from the two prompters positioned beside the podium.

The speech was mostly a summation of the kind of events L.A. Affairs was known for, catering to the rich, famous, and total nut cases in Los Angeles and Hollywood. Really, the audience members could have read this stuff off of the company's website.

But it was just as well that all I had to do was read from the prompter because my thoughts kept bouncing back to the green room and the things Shannon had said. She'd been outraged by the prospect of Elita turning the family vacation home into a B&B, and I could really relate to that, what with Mom wanting to sell the home I was raised in. I wanted to talk to Shannon again, after my speech, but I wasn't sure she would wait around.

I noticed her then, standing in the hallway to the green room, staring at me. She didn't look as if she'd calmed down any. In fact, she looked more upset. Then I realized she was rising on her toes, leaning left, then right, as if trying to spot something. Casually, as if it were part of my presentation, I glanced behind me and saw the mobile kitchen that would be moved into position at center stage that Rosalind would use for her cooking demo.

An idea zapped my brain, then another one zinged through, and my thoughts started darting around like a squirrel in traffic. Things fell into place: Shannon and her sisters objecting to Elita turning the family home into a B&B; Shannon not knowing Elita would be at the conference until she saw her name on the list of swag vendors by the messenger bag display; the stolen bags; the anonymous tip; the missing swag; Shannon's outrage at seeing Rosalind in the green room and learning she'd do a cooking demo promoting the B&B.

A weird kind of sadness swept over me—not the best thing to happen during a speech. All I could think about was my mom selling the house, Shannon and her sisters losing their childhood vacation home. All of that family stuff—gone.

So I did the unthinkable. I couldn't help myself—even with Priscilla and Edie eyeballing me.

I went off-script.

"L.A. Affairs doesn't simply stage events," I said.

Priscilla's eyes got big. Edie braced herself. I kept going.

"We make memories. Memories for families to keep, to treasure forever, no matter what the future brings." I added a thank-you and stepped back from the podium. Applause rose.

I exited the stage. Jack hurried forward and offered his hand as I walked down the stairs. He gave me a wink. Nice.

I stretched up. He leaned down.

"I know who murdered Elita," I whispered.

CHAPTER FOURTEEN

I hurried into the green room, Jack close behind.

Right away I spotted Shannon confronting Rosalind. Her voice was low but I saw the tight, angry expression on her face. Rosalind looked stunned, as did everyone else in the room.

"Wait here," I said to Jack.

I knew I had to handle this myself, if I was going to confirm my suspicion. The presence of Jack—a stranger—would cause her to clam up.

"I understand," I said to Shannon, inserting myself between her and Rosalind.

Shannon's angry gaze landed on me.

"You don't want Rosalind to do the cooking demo," I said. "You don't want any attention drawn to Elita's B&B."

"It isn't *Elita's*." Shannon voice shook with rage. "It belongs to *us*. My dad. My mom. My sisters. My sisters' kids. Not *her*."

I glimpsed Jack nearby, watching.

"I get it," I said, using my I-really-understand voice because really, I did. "You don't want guests—strangers—in the home that belongs to your family."

"My mom decorated that house. Gorgeous furnishings. Antiques. She selected everything with love to make it perfect for our family." Tears pooled in Shannon's eyes. "Those are *her* things. *Our* things. Then Elita—who has the taste level of a cow and the business sense of a gerbil—just waltzes in and takes over, and wants to leave everything in the house for *strangers* to use."

I felt slightly sick to my stomach. No way could I tolerate that, either.

"You must have been stunned when you saw Elita's name on the brochure itemizing the vendor swag," I said.

"I couldn't believe she was actually going ahead with the B&B," Shannon said, her anger rising. "She didn't even tell me or my sisters. Not a word."

"So you hid the messenger bags in the stockroom, slipped in later and took out the swag that included the B&B opening, then made the anonymous tip so the bags could be recovered for the giveaway today," I said. "You even hid the vendor swag brochures that belonged beside the display bag so Zander couldn't replenish them."

"I had to do something," Shannon said. "I couldn't let her open that B&B."

Applause drifted in from the banquet room. The next speaker had been introduced.

"You tried to talk to Elita, didn't you?" I said. "Monday night. After you read the B&B listing on the vendor swag brochure. You waited for her at the labyrinth exit."

Shannon clamped her mouth shut and drew herself up. "I don't know what you're talking about."

"You waited until she came out. You wanted to talk to her, out there, where it was quiet. You tried to make her understand how you and your sisters felt, and get her to forget opening the B&B," I said, then added a total lie. "You were seen out there."

She blanched, then color rose in her cheeks. "Well, yes. I did go out there. But just to talk to her. I had to convince her. I had to make her understand how my sisters and I felt. That house is *ours*. My sisters have kids. They want to take them there in summers, just like we used to do."

My brother and sister flashed in my head, and how I'd felt about handling things in their absence to keep Mom from selling the house.

"But Elita wouldn't listen?" I asked.

"She was completely unreasonable. She kept insisting it was *her* house—and it wasn't."

"Things got heated," I said. "You had to stop her. You grabbed the shovel."

"Only to frighten her," Shannon insisted. "But she wouldn't shut up—"

Shannon stopped. Her gaze swept the room.

"Where's Rosalind?" she demanded, panic rising in her voice.

I looked around, too. I didn't see her.

"She's not going to do that demonstration," Shannon swore. "She's not going to announce to everyone that she's cooking at the B&B. Not after everything I've done to keep it from opening."

A ripple of laughter drifted in from the banquet room.

"No!" Shannon dashed across the room and into the hallway.

"Jack! Stop her!" I called.

He ran after her. I followed, not making such good time in my skirt and pumps, and got into the banquet room in time to see Shannon climbing the steps onto the stage. Rosalind was behind the mobile kitchen, talking to the audience as she stirred a pot on the stove top.

Shannon barreled across the stage. Commotion broke out in the audience. Jack took the steps two at time. I hurried behind him.

Rosalind noticed us. She gasped and backed away.

Shannon grabbed a frying pan and swung it at Rosalind, but Jack was faster. He blocked her arm and wrenched the pan away. Shannon froze, stunned. She looked around, as if she couldn't understand where she was or what was happening.

I touched her arm and leaned close.

"Go with Jack," I whispered. "He'll take care of you. I'll be right there."

Jack caught her arm and led her off of the stage. Rosalind stood there, confused and stunned.

I grasped her hand and led her to the podium.

"That, ladies and gentlemen, was an excellent demonstration of the security services available from Jack Bishop," I said, then gestured to Rosalind. "And a special thank-you to Rosalind Russo for helping out."

Applause broke out. I headed for the green room.

***

"Here. You deserve it," Kayla said, and passed me a glass of wine.

We were in the green room and I was starting to come down from everything that had happened. Other guys from Jack's team had fallen in with him and escorted Shannon out of the banquet room, taking her to the Severin security office. I figured the homicide detectives were on their way and would take over.

"Your speech was lovely. I nearly teared up at the end." Mindy blushed. "I'm feeling kind of emotional."

"Mindy's got a hot date tonight," Kayla said.

Her cheeks grew redder. "With Carlos."

"It's Charles," Kayla told her.

"That's great," I said and I meant it, now that I no longer suspected him of murder.

"Oh, look who's here," Mindy said. "It's Patty and Edna."

I followed her gaze and saw Priscilla and Edie walk into the room.

"Oh my God," Kayla murmured. "Brace yourselves."

I sipped the wine—okay, it was more than a sip—and set the glass aside, thinking it was better to keep a clear head.

"Haley, about the speech." Priscilla made a prune-face, then smiled. "It was fantastic."

"The part you added at the end about L.A. Affairs making memories," Edie said. "It hit the right note. I could see the audience really connected with you."

"The tie-in with the security company was a stroke of genius," Priscilla said. "It showed yet another dimension to our events."

"Staging that confrontation during the celebrity chef's cooking demo was genius," Edie said. "It's all over social media already."

"Linking us to Rosalind Russo was brilliant," Priscilla said. "You two definitely have a connection. Do you think you could get her to agree to cook for some of our events?"

I'd accused Rosalind of murdering Elita and I was pretty sure I was the last person she'd want to work with, so what could I say but, "Sure."

"We've received a number of calls and email throughout the week from vendors here at the conference," Priscilla said. "You and Kayla and Mindy have made an outstanding impression on everyone."

Priscilla glanced at Edie and got a slight head nod in return. "So, Haley, you've done a wonderful job representing us here at the conference, elevating our profile and bringing positive attention to L.A Affairs. We're anxious to hear your ideas on continuing to move forward."

My first thought was to suggest firing Nadine—but that was way too selfish. I'd deal with her myself on Monday morning.

Something to look forward to.

"One thing comes to mind immediately," I said. "The entire office would benefit from additional organization, so I think everyone should be given a Titan messenger bag."

Priscilla and Edie both gasped.

"What a wonderful idea," Edie declared.

"I'll get right on it," Priscilla said.

"How about some wine to celebrate?" Kayla said, and gathered glasses from the buffet table.

I eased away as Kayla poured and Edie and Priscilla continued to rave about our efforts to promote L.A. Affairs this week, grabbed my handbag and left the green room. I was happy to bask in the glory of a job well done, a murder solved, and messenger bags recovered, but I needed a break from it.

The main corridor was nearly empty as I crossed the lobby and headed toward the exit. I'd almost made it to fresh air and sunshine when my cell phone buzzed. Mom was calling.

Sadness swept over me, knowing what she was about to tell me. Multiple offers, an excited buyer, a quick escrow. I'd let down my brother and sister—but at least I hadn't resorted to murder, as Shannon had done.

"I'm so insulted," Mom declared when I answered.

I couldn't even ask a what-the-heck question before she went on.

"Multiple offers, indeed." She huffed. "Tear-downs. All of them."

My senses jumped to high alert.

"All the buyers wanted to tear down the house?" I asked. Actually, I might have shouted that.

"Can you imagine? This beautiful house with all of its charm, its character, its dignity, torn down and replaced by one of those contemporary monstrosities? Obviously, today's buyers have absolutely no taste."

"So you're not selling?" I asked.

"Not until a home of this grandeur is better appreciated," Mom said. "I cancelled the listing and fired my agent on the spot."

I didn't really notice what else Mom said as we ended the call, I was smiling so big. I left the conference center as I tapped out messages to my brother and sister, letting them know that yet another of Mom's disastrous plans had been foiled.

Outside the sun was bright in the cloudless sky, the breeze gentle. Two cars pulled up to the valet. A helicopter descended toward the helipad. I headed for the labyrinth.

The moments I'd spent there with Jack played in my mind. I'd been so ready to leave, to go with him. I was sure it meant something, something I'd face at another time.

For now, I was relieved that Elita's murder was solved, the messenger bags were recovered, and I still had my job. Mom wasn't selling the house. Mindy had a new man in her life. Jack's business reputation had been restored. I was getting a Titan messenger bag.

All and all, it had been a heck of a week. I wanted nothing more than to go home, load up on everything chocolate I could find, and spent my weekend mindlessly relaxing.

But first I wanted to call Detective Shuman with an update on Elita's murder. I tapped his name on my contact list and he answered right away.

"I found the killer," I announced. "She's in custody."

"Awesome," Shuman said. "I want to hear all about it. I'm free. Meet me. I'll have a frappie waiting for you."

Up ahead on the walkway I spotted Jack. He shifted, his gaze caressed me, and a guess-what-I'm-thinking grin pulled at his lips as he lifted a tray filled with mocha frappuccinos.

Before I could react, my cell phone chimed. I text message from Liam appeared that read, "Surprise! Look behind you!"

I turned and saw Liam leaving the valet, walking toward me with a Starbucks cup in his hand.

The helicopter touched down. The door opened and a guy carrying a mocha frappuccino got out, and—oh my God, it was Ty. Oh, crap.

The End

Dear Reader:

I hope you enjoyed this novella, and cordially invite you to check out the other books in my Haley Randolph series. You might also like my Dana Mackenzie series featuring an amateur sleuth who takes on the faceless corporation she works for while solving murders.

If you're up for adding a little romance to your life, I also write historical romance novels under the pen name Judith Stacy.

More information is available at DorothyHowellNovels.com and JudithStacy.com. Stay up to date by visiting my Facebook page DorothyHowellNovels. If you're wondering what I look like, check out my Instagram page DorothyHowellNovels.

Thanks for adding my books to your library and recommending me to your friends and family.

Happy reading!

Dorothy

Dorothy Howell is the author of 43 novels. She writes the Haley Randolph and the Dana Mackenzie mysteries series, and writes historical romance novels under the pen name Judith Stacy. Dorothy lives with her family in Southern California.